SPIRIT
MARKED

StarHaven Sanctuary: Book Two

Tera Lyn Cortez

Original cover art by Melony Paradise
Paradise Cover Designs

DEDICATION

For all the friends who have stood by me when I struggled, when I doubted myself, and when I needed you most. I appreciate you more than words can ever express. Lots of love to all of you!

CHAPTER ONE

Sweat poured off me, mingling with tears that I no longer attempted to blink back. My fingers curled into the dry earth as I knelt on the forest floor in the clearing, calling on Mother Nature for help even after she had failed to help me the first thousand times I begged her. Activating my wolf genes proved to be more difficult than either Isaiah or I had imagined. So far, nothing we tried brought forth my ability to shift.

"Push through it. Think of your wolf as your

other half. Let her be in charge and come forward."
Isaiah stood in front of me, giving instructions.

Unlike the others in the pack, my wolf did not
appear to have a separate personality. I didn't hear
her voice in my head or feel her presence. The elders
predicted that because I bore only half the genes of a
regular werewolf that I may not have a spirit wolf,
that perhaps my body would accept the shift of form
but remain wholly my own. It explained why I
couldn't shift with ease, because I had no other magic
to help me. No wolf inside me wanted to come into
the physical world. I simply asked my body to do
something abnormal, even if it was capable of doing
so.

"I CAN'T DO IT!" My voice cracked on the final
word.

Falling flat to the dirt, pine needles and pebbles
bit into my cheek and forehead before I drug my arms
to rest on each other and cradled my head within
them, hiding my face and letting the tears fall to the
forest floor. The word tired couldn't cover the state of
my body. Exhausted didn't come close either. If a
word existed for mostly dead, that would be the one I

would use.

Isaiah's footsteps stopped just inches from my head. He didn't speak, and he didn't touch me. He just waited. And I let him wait. In spite of his unwavering faith that I would be able to shift, I didn't believe it to be possible. If I could have done it, the transformation would have happened by now. We'd tried everything. And every single thing had failed.

Finally, he got impatient. "Leah. Look at me. Please?" His knees cracked as he crouched in front of me.

Sniffling, I drug my sleeves across my face before looking up at him, but made no attempt to rise. I had nothing left in me to work with.

"Let's take a break. We'll figure it out."

My unsteady exhale blew out with enough force to send the topmost layer of pine needles tumbling away from me. "No. We won't. I can't shift. We have to accept that. We keep trying and nothing has been successful. I have almost no magic any more, and my wolf genes are worse than useless. I'm as good as worthless."

"Stop saying that. You are not worthless. We may

not have all the answers, but we will find them. Get up."

When I ignored him, he positioned himself over me and wrapped his hands around my waist, lifting me to my feet. Briefly, I toyed with the idea of sinking right back to the ground, but remained standing. Getting back home and into my bed would happen faster if I walked and didn't crawl.

"I'm ready to go home and call it a day. Maybe I can find a spell in one of the books that will help me tap into my other half."

The comment came out half-heartedly, as I'd already been through many of the books and hadn't run across anything that could be even remotely helpful. My hope was that if I sounded like I would be doing something useful, then he wouldn't try to come up with another solution.

"Do you want to walk over to the beach and have a picnic dinner? It could help you relax."

A hopeful expression crossed his face, making me feel guilty for wanting to say no. The sigh escaped before I could catch it.

"No, I really don't. I'm sorry. I just want to go to

bed. Do you want to come back for dinner before you head home? We both need to eat."

He let out a matching sigh. "Only if you really want me to. I get the feeling you really want to be alone."

He tensed as my hand landed on his arm. "I'm sorry. I'm just exhausted and defeated. I feel empty without my magic. I feel guilty because we let the evil spirit escape. I feel betrayed because my mother let me live my whole life in the dark about my true nature. I have all these feelings that are raging like a hurricane and I'm just a dilapidated little shack, perched on the beach with no storm protection, waiting to be swept out to sea."

His amber eyes darkened. "*I* am your storm protection. Let me be your foundation, your anchor, even your storm shutters. Whatever you need me to be, just let me help you."

"That's half the problem! I don't *know* what I need you to be. I can't even decide on a role for myself, much less anyone else right now."

My embarrassment at being so out of control of my emotions kept my gaze rooted firmly on the ground. Instead of asking me to face him, he grabbed my hand and began leading me back down the trail toward the house. Instead of resisting, I let him lead me home.

As we passed under the large tree at the edge of the clearing, angry chatter jarred me from my thoughts. The two tiny chipmunks sat on the lowest branch, scolding me. They still hadn't forgiven me for trapping them in the bubble and then forgetting about them for a while. To be fair, I hadn't forgiven them for chewing up my books either, so we were at a stalemate.

My feet stopped walking, and I looked up. "Look. I'm *sorry*, okay? I am. There, I apologized. And frankly, you owe me an apology, too. So you can just sit up there and be quiet."

Isaiah had to take a couple of quick steps to catch up as I stalked toward the porch. "Did you really just yell at a couple of rodents?" The mirth in his tone was unmistakable.

"You shut it. I've had a really shitty couple of days, and I will not be lectured by a 'couple of rodents' every time I leave my house. My patience for everyone else's shit is gone." I looked at him, not bothering to school my expression. "And that goes for you, too, mister." I dug my pointer finger into his chest for emphasis.

He pressed his lips together, tightening them to suppress a smile, and drew his brows down into a serious expression. "Better?"

"Hmph."

My dignified stalking across the clearing was impeded by a wayward shoelace and my innate ability to fumble and fall over any little thing. Arms pinwheeling, I somehow managed to make an incredibly ungraceful pirouette, landing flat on my back with my hip throbbing and the back of my head stinging. Every other part of me just ached.

"Are you okay?" The quaver in his voice gave away his laughter, as much as he attempted to hide it.

"Argh." A groan was the best answer I could produce.

His face swam into focus above me. "Let me help you up." He grabbed my hand and pulled me to my feet. "Come on, you really do need some sleep."

We slipped through the back door and he guided

me to a seat at the table, which I sank into with another groan. Dinner sat in dishes on the stove, but my mother was nowhere in sight. Thankfully. Our relationship had been deteriorating, and I didn't have the emotional stamina to do anything about it right at that moment. I didn't know if I would any time soon.

"Want me to make you a plate?" He stood in front of the stove, waiting for me to agree before serving up a plate.

"Might as well. I haven't got it in me to cook, and I hate to waste food."

He glanced my way. "It's not as if she is going to try to poison you, you know."

Ignoring him, I accepted the meal as he sat it in front of me. "I don't suppose you could grab me some Tylenol, too? Please?"

He dropped the two small pills in my hand as he sat down with his own plate. We ate in silence, both focused on our own thoughts. I noticed him watching me from the corner of his eye, fork paused in mid air.

"What?"

"Do you regret it? Regret breaking the curse? Ultimately, that's what cost you your magic."

My head wobbled. "No. What cost me my magic is being stupid enough to be sucked in by the dark spirit's illusion that she was my aunt. I should have known that Aimee would never have hidden something near the stream where she couldn't keep it protected."

My disgust at myself hung in the pit of my stomach like a brick, erasing my appetite. Bile crawled up and threatened to bring up the few bites of food I'd already eaten with it. I asked myself on the hour how I could have possibly been so foolish. So far, I hadn't come up with a reasonable answer.

"But if you hadn't been helping us, you wouldn't have been there in the first place."

"I'll never regret helping you guys." I set my fork down and took a deep breath. "Do I miss my magic? Absolutely. And I am going to try my damnedest to get it back, somehow. But removing the curse was the right thing to do. I needed to do that for you and the pack. I wouldn't take it back even if I could."

"Your mom thinks she can help you regain your magic. Why don't you let her try at least? It couldn't hurt."

The chair scraped against the floor as I pushed it back, fuming as I dumped the rest of my dinner in the trash and then carried the dish to the sink. "Because I don't trust her!" I shouted the words at him. "My entire life has been a lie. She lied directly to my face even when confronted with the truth. Who knows what she might try? What if she can block my access to it forever?"

"Do you really believe I would do that? To my own daughter?"

My mother's voice from the hallway startled me, resulting in the dinner plate I had been holding crashing into the cast iron sink and shattering. Isaiah grabbed the trashcan and drug it over.

"Let me help you."

"I've got it." I turned to look at my mother as I reached into the sink to grab the pieces. "How the hell should I know? You've already done everything possible to ensure that I grew up completely oblivious to my heritage! No wonder my father's identity was such a touchy subject. Hell, even to this day, you won't tell me who he is."

"I thought I was doing what was best for you!"

"Yeah? And how do I know you won't try to do whatever it is that you think is best for me now? You seem to think you know best, even when you haven't got a damn clue."

My hands clenched as I seethed, digging the sharp edge of the plate into my palm. Until Isaiah reached for me, I didn't even notice.

"You're bleeding. Let go of the plate, Leah." He opened my fingers and gently removed the shard from my hand.

My mother continued to watch from the doorway, her hand resting against the jamb, lip quivering. Turning my back to her, I continued to drop the china pieces into the trashcan with my free hand while Isaiah pressed a towel to my other hand.

"You might need some stitches. Perhaps-"

"It will heal. Don't worry about it."

By the time I turned to face him, she had disappeared, moving away as silently as she had approached. I sighed in relief. My self-control slipped every time we communicated, and I just didn't have it in me to cope at the moment.

Isaiah pulled me into his arms. The support

melted me, and I sagged against him. I hurt so badly. Physically. Emotionally. Spiritually. My very soul ached, and I had no clue how to put an end to it.

"Thank you." The whisper was soft, but I knew he heard me.

"No thanks necessary. Let me tuck you in before I head back for the night."

"I'd rather walk you out. I feel like taking one last look at the moon before I head to bed."

He kissed my forehead and turned toward the door. As we stepped out onto the porch, he grinned and nudged me, steering my attention to the little table. Laying there in the exact spot I used to leave crackers for my little friends was a pile of trinkets. Small floral blooms, a pine cone, and two beautiful pebbles.

"How's that for an apology?" I smiled at the gesture. "Hang on, I need to get them something too."

Scooping up my treasures, I went into the house. Chocolate chip cookies and crackers filled the bowl I had grabbed from the cupboard. As an afterthought, I threw a couple of grapes into the mix as well. Returning to the porch, I set the bowl out for them to find.

"There."

Isaiah and I stood for a minute in silence, listening to the sounds of the sanctuary. It seemed deceptively peaceful. Somewhere out there, the evil spirit roamed, biding her time. As I thought of her, the hairs on my neck stood up.

"She's out there."

Isaiah nodded. "We'll find her. And we'll destroy her when we do."

"I have got to get my magic back. Somehow. I must learn to shift and restore my mark."

Keeping our voices low, we murmured to each other, not wanting to draw attention to ourselves.

"We'll figure something out. I promise."

It was my turn to nod. "Be careful on your way back, okay? Something feels off tonight."

"I promise."

He slipped into the trees, blending into the shadows as if he'd never been there. A shiver ran down my spine. The feeling of foreboding that coursed through my body left me chilled. Something big was coming.

CHAPTER TWO

The back door hadn't even latched shut when my mother pounced. "We need to have a chat, Leah. And you are going to listen to me."

"Excuse me? I am not seven years old, and you don't get to tell me what to do any more." Anger bubbled up through my insides and I could feel myself on the verge of foaming at the mouth.

"Listen here, Miss I'm-Such-a-Grown-Up. Adults listen even when they are afraid they won't like what they hear. It's one of the basic principals of maturity."

She stared at me, hands on her hips, waiting for a response. My own hand remained on the doorknob, half of me tempted to open it once more and walk right back out. The other half of me, the slightly more "mature" half, wanted to hash things out with her. Now seemed as good a time as any to do so.

"Okay. Go ahead." I waved my free hand vaguely in her direction, indicating she should get on with it.

Her shoulders relaxed, and she crossed the kitchen to the fridge. "I'm getting a glass of wine. Would you like one?"

The offer caught me off guard, as my mother had never been much of a drinker. But I accepted anyway. Might as well dull the edge of what was about to be a very unpleasant interaction. Perhaps it would help us both to work through some of our issues.

Wine glasses in hand, we went to the living room and settled onto the sofa, fireplace already burning and giving off steady warmth. Taking one of Aimee's favorite throw pillows, I settled it in my lap, hugging it close to me for comfort as I ran my fingers over the mocha-colored satin. Thinking of her sitting here in the same corner of the couch and making the same motions as we had heart to heart talks in the past, grabbed my despair and drug it to the surface. Oh, how I needed her now.

My mom inhaled deeply before beginning. "I know you are angry with me. And I understand where you are coming from, I really do. You have every right to be mad."

Her admission shocked me, coming from someone usually so defensive about their choices. She rarely admitted to wrong-doing and defended her decisions with the tenacity of a wolverine going after a meal. I nodded in acknowledgment but didn't speak.

"I want to help you now, in any way I can. If we don't work together, my mother's spirit will best us all. And we cannot let our petty family squabble impact the rest of the sanctuary, or the world, like that. If we don't stop her, nobody else will be able to. She will continue to grow in strength and power, wreaking havoc wherever she goes. No matter how angry you are with me, I know you don't want that to happen."

I mulled her words over, trying to decide on the best response before answering. She had a point. "You are right. I don't want that. But I don't trust you anymore. You may have saved my life, but had you been on my side from the beginning, you never would have needed to come to my aid. She admitted I had the potential to be so much more powerful than she ever was. But I didn't have that ability because you stole it from me. Your choices got us to where we stand today."

"And I will spend the rest of my days paying for my choices. As will you if you choose not to accept what help I can offer. Should you choose not to accept that help, we may have very few days left to ruminate over our decisions anyways."

Damn her for being reasonable when I wanted to be angry. "What do you have in mind?"

"I'd like to try two things. One, I believe I can lend you some of my power through an amulet. While I have never been overly strong in my magic, it would give you a little something to work with for now, and may kick-start your own magic if you can find a way to make it grow."

My mouth dropped at her suggestion. She just offered to limit her own abilities in order to give me back a bit of my own. After trying to keep me from it all these years. She didn't wait for me to answer before continuing.

"Two, I know you have been trying to activate your wolf genes. While I have very little experience with that, I would like to try and perform the same ritual on you that you used to bring Isaiah's human side forward for that first time. Perhaps between the two of us, we can force the change. It should be easier for future shifts once your body has accepted the new form."

If I thought her first suggestion shocked me, nothing could have prepared me for this. She'd rendered me well and truly speechless, perhaps for the first time in my entire life. My ears rang in confusion. My eyes blinked repeatedly, as if they, too, were having trouble processing the message.

"Are you serious?" My astonishment had limited the vocabulary I had available for a response.

"Very. I meant it when I said I would do anything to help you. I would give my own life to see you succeed."

"That isn't necessary, thank you very much. Let's

not get over-excited here. I will, however, accept your offers on one condition."

She rolled her eyes, but said nothing.

"No more secrets. No more lies. I get to decide what is best for me."

"I'll do my best not to interfere. Remember, I carried you within my own body. It's difficult to not try and do what you think would be most beneficial for your own flesh and blood, even long after they need you no more."

My gut told me we would find ourselves on opposite sides of an opinion more than ever in the coming days, but she was right when she pointed out I needed all the help I could get. I couldn't bear the thought of hitting the point that I'd wished I had taken her up on her offer, only to have it be too late.

"When can we start?"

She reached into the pocket of her jeans and pulled out a large garnet ring. The cushion cut stone had to be at least five carats, surrounded by an intricate band. The reflection of the flames from the fireplace brought the ring to life in her hands.

"Wear this on the ring finger of your left hand.

Betroth yourself to the magic within it. The stone is said to have numerous properties. Garnet is widely known as a protective gem, as well as a bringer of balance. They also have healing properties. I chose it in hopes that, coupled with my magic, it could help you to heal your own."

She took my hand and began murmuring words, barely in an audible voice. My ears couldn't make out the chant, could barely discern the syllables. As she finished, she slipped the ring on my hand. The infusion of magic was instantaneous. Using what I had learned from the books when I first discovered their existence, I opened myself up and drew in as much as I could.

The rush of it hit me, making me wonder if this was the feeling drug addicts chased as they got high. If so, I could clearly see their desire to repeat it.

"It feels different from my own magic. I can certainly tell it's borrowed, not owned."

"Yes, it will take some getting used to, and will not give you all the advantages of your own magic. But, for now, at least you aren't totally helpless."

"Are we going to try to shift tonight?" Now that

we had started, I wanted to keep moving forward.

"If you want to, we can. If you want to get a good night's sleep and try it in the morning, we can do that too. I believe I know which spell you used."

"Let's just try. If we can't make it work, we can try again tomorrow after I get some rest."

"Okay, follow me."

She headed down the hall and through the door that led to the basement. After descending the stairs, she stood in the center of the room for a moment, as if trying to get her bearings. Tapping her finger against her lips, she studied the space around her. After a moment, she walked over to an old wooden armoire, put her shoulder against it and shoved.

With a scraping sound, the hefty piece of furniture moved to the right, revealing a solid-looking door. Runes and symbols covered the surface. It opened on hinges that made no sound, as if they had been oiled recently. The sight behind the door took my breath away.

"Shoes and socks off." She wasted no time entering the room.

My surprise slowed my actions as I followed suit.

Goosebumps raced across my skin as my bare feet touched the cool, rough concrete of the basement floor. My Converse held my socks, laces still tied off to the side of the door frame.

Entering the hidden room was like walking into a lush jungle. Despite the lack of natural sunlight, beautiful plants covered the walls and hung from the ceiling. The cement of the basement floor stopped at the doorjamb and nothing but loamy earth touched the soles of my feet as I followed my mother inside. She closed the door behind us as I continued to drink it all in.

Inhaling as deeply as I could, I took in the scents around me. A small well occupied the far corner of the room, built of blue agate stones. The water burbled quietly, as if rising from great depths. As I looked down into the crystal clear water, it seemed to go on forever.

"What is this place?" My voice barely rose above a whisper.

"This is our family's connection with the reserve itself. I worried that without Aimee here to tend it, we might have found it struggling, but it seems to be doing fine, for now. This will be the best place to try to bring forth your wolf form, and also to reconnect with your mark."

My fingertips brushed the leaf a vine with reverence. The slightest touch and I could feel the texture of the structures within the green skin. The existence of this place left me in awe.

"Sit on the earth. Make a connection, as true as you can manage. Close your eyes and feel the energy here."

Following her instruction, I sat, digging my fingers and toes into the remarkably warm earth. I let the smells tickle my senses and block out all other thoughts. Minutes passed in silence. My mother sat in front of me, our knees touching. She took my hands, folding them into her own.

She began the chant I had worked so hard to memorize not that long before, the words reverberating in my mind as she spoke them. I could feel her magic washing over me, digging deep and coaxing mine to come forward. I could also feel the resistance.

She pulled while I pushed, silently begging

mother nature to please let this side of me come forth to be recognized. My other half deserved its turn to run free. My body began to ache. My head throbbed. The sensation of tension pulled along my muscles and bones. Sweat beaded and ran down my body. My skin took on the feeling of a million centipedes dancing along its surface. And still my mother chanted.

Her voice grew in volume and power as she insisted my body do what she commanded, in spite of its reluctance to do so. The pain increased, drawing out a guttural groan I could no longer hold in. Every cell in my body caught fire, and it burned. Tears streamed down my face as I prayed that all of this pain wouldn't be for naught.

My hands squeezed hers as I scrabbled for any hint of comfort. Despite my crushing grip, she remained relaxed and focused, the words of the incantation never wavering. I began to wonder if it would ever end.

Pain ripped through my body, trapping me in an instant where I was certain my soul had been torn from the flesh that housed it and incinerated. Every cell writhed in agony. At the edge of my sanity, when

I was certain I could take no more, it stopped, and an all-consuming inky blackness took its place.

"Leah. Leah. Can you hear me?"

I could feel her shaking me, but couldn't bring myself to respond. My limbs refused to obey my brain's commands. A blink was the best I could do to let her know I wasn't dead-yet. Managing to focus my vision took effort, and when I did, the look on her face astounded me. She looked horrified.

"I thought I had killed you. How do you feel?"

I tried to answer her, but nothing came out. My throat was too parched for my vocal chords to work. Planning to hoist myself into a sitting position, I attempted to get my arms underneath me, despite their painful weakness. As they buckled underneath me, I gasped. My arms weren't weak at all. My front legs were.

I looked at my mother for guidance. We had done it. I tried to speak to her and discovered I could not. Of course I couldn't; wolves don't have a voice box. The realization led to panic.

She must have seen it in my eyes, because she reached out and laid a hand on my shoulder in an effort to calm me. "It's okay, just rest for a minute."

Using the telepathy I had learned with Isaiah, I reached out to her, only to find silence at the other end. My mother was not capable of conversing in that way. I had managed to effectively cut off all means of communicating without a back-up plan.

Wishing myself back into my human form got me nowhere. I lay on my side, panting. I could feel an abnormally long tongue lolling about in my mouth. A useless tongue that couldn't even form words.

While the scenario could be largely seen as a success based on my original desire, it dawned on me that I had gotten my wolf form to come to the surface, but I had no idea how to put it back. What the hell was I supposed to do now?

CHAPTER THREE

My attempts to communicate with my mother went unanswered. I tried to call for Isaiah, but that channel seemed blocked to me as well. On top of my mental panic, the forcing of the shift had drained my body of all physical energy. I couldn't even force this four-legged heap of auburn fur to get up. My mom absently stroked my head as she tried to reassure me.

"Stop petting me!"

While the words seemed to echo off the sides of my skull, bouncing around like a pinball machine, she paid me no mind, totally oblivious to my attempts to speak to her. If she didn't stop patting me soon, I was going to bite her. I'd find the energy for that somewhere.

"Can you get up yet? Or switch back?"

I shook my head back and forth.

"No? Hm. When you feel like you have the energy, we can at least get you upstairs, where you might be more comfortable. You may be petite, but I doubt I could carry you up there without one of us getting hurt."

"Wow. Thanks a bunch, Mom."

My inability to speak to my mother made sense, but I didn't understand why I could not connect with Isaiah. The connection between us shouldn't have been lost just because my physical form was different; I had the same brain. Every time I attempted to get all four legs underneath me so that I could stand, weakness overtook me. My body was so worn out from the force of the change that I couldn't even get out of the dirt I was laying in.

The last thing I wanted was to fall asleep here in the dirt, but I wasn't sure I was going to have much choice. My mother was right, she couldn't carry me up the stairs. If I couldn't get a hold of Isaiah in some way, nobody was going to be carrying me anywhere. So far, my pride still had a good enough grip that I was not going to be crawling out the door on my furry belly.

Food might help, but I had no way of explaining to my mother that I needed to eat. Anger at myself bubbled in my belly since I hadn't thought enough about what would happen if we were actually successful to prepare ahead of time. Had I done that, I might not be wallowing where I was at the moment. My impatience had gotten the better of me and now I was stuck paying the price.

"Should I go upstairs and get a bowl so I can at least give you some water?" my mother asked.

I did my best to nod my head, unsure of whether I would actually be able to drink from a bowl. Having never been a canine before, my ability to use this physical form would surely be limited. As I waited for her to return, I heard a knock at the back door. My heart jumped. Could it be Isaiah? Had he somehow heard me? Nobody else would be knocking on the door at this time of night.

Thanks to my current pair of ears, I heard his voice as soon as my mother opened the back door, and I let out an unintentional whine, instantly embarrassed and thankful they weren't down here to hear me. His footsteps thundered down the stairs as my mom directed him to where I lay. He stopped dead in the doorway when he caught sight of me, leaving me to wonder if something was wrong with my wolf. Was I deformed? Hideously ugly?

"Leah?"

Another embarrassing whine. I couldn't help it, though. My telepathy didn't work and I couldn't speak English at that moment. He stepped over the doorway, coming to an abrupt halt as soon as he made it fully inside. His brow furrowed and his eyes narrowed. He took a step backwards into the basement, then stepped forward again. After doing this a couple of times, he turned toward my mother.

"Is this room warded somehow?"

My mom nodded. "It's private. It is our family's personal connection to the magic of the reserve. Outside magic is not allowed."

Understanding dawned on his face as he turned to me. "Hey there. Doing okay?"

The snort that came out in response made him laugh.

"I'm going to pick you up and carry you out of here, okay? The protections in place are the reason you can't hear me and vice-versa. Once we get you back into the house, I should have no problem hearing you. Ready?"

The whine came again, and this time I didn't care because I just wanted someone to understand me. Had I been able to garner the energy to walk out of here on my own, I would have been able to call him here myself. I very much wanted to know what brought him to our door in the middle of the night, or whatever time it was.

Once we cleared the threshold, our connection rang through loud and clear. "Oh, thank the goddess! I can't tell you how panicked I have been. How did you know to come?"

He chuckled. "I got worried when you disappeared from my head. Even when we aren't actively talking, I can feel the pathway between us. I must have been sleeping when it originally cut off, but I woke to find it gone and knew something must be up. I waited for a bit to see if it would come back, because I didn't want to interfere if you had cut it off on purpose. When it didn't, I needed to at least come check on you."

We'd made it up the basement stairs with no problem and he turned down the hall to my room. Positioning me on the bed with my head on the pillow, he looked me over, then sat in the chair beside the bed. Feeling self-conscious about my new form, I lifted my head to stare down at myself, getting my first view of what I looked like as a wolf.

Holy shit. My mom's idea had worked. She managed to force me to turn from human into a wolf. All I could do was pray now that someone could force me to turn back. I didn't want to stay this way forever. Tomorrow might even be too long. Not having control over my form made me twitchy.

"I'm so glad you did. I about had a heart attack when I realized I couldn't communicate with anybody at all. And I seem to be stuck. I can't turn back."

"You may just need food and rest. The first shift

is a huge undertaking, especially when it is forced and not naturally occurring. Don't panic yet. We'll figure it out. Are you hungry?"

"Starved, but I'm not sure I can bring myself to eat out of a bowl, like a dog. No offense."

He burst out laughing. "None taken. It takes some getting used to. How about a sandwich or something? I'll even give you bites."

My stomach rumbled in response. "That would be amazing. Thank you. What would I do without you?"

"You'd figure it out." He stood up. "Rest. I'll be back in a few minutes."

My vision wavered from exhaustion, calling attention to the subtle change in the way my eyes worked in this form. Colors were bland and somewhat degraded, although I was unsure if I would have noticed had I not already known what the colors in my room looked like. Letting my head flop back onto the pillow, I closed my eyes, intending to rest just until Isaiah came back with my food. Apparently, my body had other ideas.

By the time my eyes opened again, the sun had risen and beams of light filtered through the partially open curtains. My mouth tasted like a dirty gym sock, reinforcing my theory that pretty much every creature could get morning breath. Isaiah was nowhere to be seen, and I got the bright idea to get out of bed myself, somehow forgetting that I hadn't learned to use this new body yet.

My struggle to get my legs under me led to a slide straight off the edge of the mattress and onto the wood floor. Each leg went a different direction, leaving me sprawled on my belly with my nose facing the bathroom. Oh geez, the bathroom. The sight of it reminded me I needed to empty my bladder and I sure as hell wasn't doing it in the yard.

I let out a frustrated growl, surprising even myself at the sound of it. At the sound of snickers, I looked up to see my mom and Isaiah standing in the doorway. My paws scrabbled to gain purchase on the slippery floor, unsuccessfully.

"Can I help you? I'll lift you up and hang onto you until you feel steady on your feet?"

"Ah, go ahead. I'm apparently not going to be able to do it myself yet."

Standing over me, he gently lifted me to a

standing position, staying close. Once all four feet bore my weight, I told him to go ahead and let go. I lift each foot in turn, attempting to figure out how to operate this current vessel for my very human mind.

"You look like a cat shaking out wet feet," my mom giggled.

I shot a glare her way, or at least tried to. "Shut up!"

Isaiah smiled. "I am not relaying that message."

"Hmph. Some help you are."

If I concentrated on one foot at a time, I was able to walk, although I staggered like a drunken sailor on a bender. My snout bounced off the door frame, bringing on a sneeze. Controlling four separate feet and watching where I was going at the same time proved harder than I expected it to be.

By some miracle, I made it to the kitchen and sat down without incident. "Okay, we need to get me back to my regular body. I have to pee."

"You know, wolves can pee too, right?" Isaiah eyed me from the chair in front of me.

"Oh, hell no. I am not going out to pee in the woods." Isaiah played go-between, repeating everything I said, so my mom knew what I worried about as well.

"Well, you had better not pee on the floor, Missy!" My mom pretended to swat me with a towel.

"Mo-om! Stop it. I am not going to pee on the floor unless you can't fix this. Then I will pee in your shoes."

Isaiah looked at me, shrugged, and relayed the message, laughing at my mom's expression.

Her mouth dropped open. "Young lady, you wouldn't dare!"

"Wanna make a bet?"

As much as I had wanted to activate my wolf genes, I already decided that being human was the way to go. I didn't think I would be capable of making the transition for long term. All I wanted out of this was for my mark to return.

Mom looked thoughtful for a moment. "I think the best place to do it would be back downstairs, where we managed to change you into this form. It's where our connection to the magic of the reserve is strongest, and I think that will be the most likely place for your mark to reappear."

I stood and headed toward the basement door, pausing at the flight of stairs. I could barely walk. How on earth would I make it down the steps without falling all the way and breaking my neck?

"Let me carry you?" Isaiah stood beside me, waiting for permission.

"Oh hell, go ahead. I'm not going to get down there any other way without hurting myself. But you put me down as soon as we are off the stairs. Please."

He did as requested and I walked over to the hidden door, waiting for my mother to open it again. Boy, did I miss having hands. And arms. And every other human part I had grown accustomed to over my twenty-seven years. The sight of my Converse on the concrete made me eager for "real" feet again.

We settled in the dirt once more, my mom sitting cross-legged in front of me. "I'm going to use the same spell as before, just focusing on your human form instead. I think it will be a little easier, as that is the form your body naturally takes." She glanced Isaiah's way. "Do not interfere for any reason. It was not a pleasant experience last time, and I don't know exactly what to expect this time. But if you interrupt me, you could kill her. Is that clear?"

His eyes widened slightly, but he nodded his agreement, leaning back against the wall a safe distance away to give us space. My mom placed her hands on my shoulders and instructed me to close my eyes and focus, just like we had done the night before. Her chanting began after a few deep breaths.

A low whine escaped as I felt the almost familiar sensation of stretching and tearing begin almost immediately. My body eagerly participated in getting itself back to normal, drinking in the magic this time instead of fighting it. The words of the spell rolled through me, and only a few short minutes later, I lay panting on the dirt floor.

Human again, and utterly naked.

CHAPTER FOUR

What the hell had happened to my clothes? Out of the corner of my eye, I saw Isaiah turn around quickly to face the door instead of staring at my bare form. He shrugged out of the sweatshirt he'd been wearing and tossed it behind him without looking my way. With a struggle, I sat up and my mom helped me to get it over my head, guiding me patiently as I tangled both arms in the sleeves in my rush to get covered.

Thankfully, the difference in our heights allowed a hip-length top for him to be a mid-thigh garment for me. Raising onto my knees, I did my best to brush the dirt from all the places you don't want it to be, but it manages to get when you are sitting down with nothing to keep it out.

"Help me up, please?"

After two very taxing experiences, I had nothing left in the tank to give. My systems were starved, so none of my muscles wanted to obey my brain. And I still needed to get to the bathroom.

"Are you sure you're ready? We can sit a few more minutes." My mom looked concerned that I wanted to get up already.

"I have to pee, remember?!" Desperation made my tone sharper than I intended it to be.

Isaiah didn't wait another minute, swooping in and scooping me up in his arms. He took the basement stairs two at a time and deposited me right inside the bathroom door, backing out and closing it behind him. Never had I been so glad to see a hunk of porcelain in my entire life. My elbows rested on my knees, giving my arms the strength they needed to support my head as I sat trying to get the motivation to stand up long after I had finished.

"Are you okay in there?" My mom's voice floated through the door. "I brought you some clothes."

Her arm snaked through the door, holding a pair of sweatpants and some socks. Reaching for them, I made the mistake of not hanging on with the other hand and lost my balance. It felt like slow motion as I pitched forward, my head connecting with the bathroom door and slamming my mom's forearm between the edge and the wall.

She yelped as I groaned, sliding myself sideways to release the pressure on her arm so she could remove it. Rolling over onto my back, I stared at the ceiling, the tiles cold against my bare cheeks. The door pushed against my leg as it cracked open.

"Are you okay? Can I help you?" Isaiah's voice floated through the crack.

The number of times I'd heard those two questions over the last day made it grate on my nerves. To be fair, though, I was not okay, and I did need help. Again.

"I doubt I can get my pants on, and there is literally no hope for me to get these socks on by myself."

The pressure on my leg increased as he tried to push it open far enough to squeeze in. I scooted slightly to the right, pressing up against the cabinet. The six-inch gap didn't give him enough room to get through.

"You're going to have to sit up or I am never going to fit through the doorway."

"Ugh. Maybe I'll just sleep here tonight, then."

He laughed out loud, the door shivering against my leg as he leaned against it for support. "Sit up lazy bones. Let me in."

"Gah... do I have to? I don't know if I can. Like, I honestly don't know if I have the strength to pull myself up. Every cell in my body aches."

"Well, here's your motivation. If I can get in there and get you dressed, then I will carry you to your bed to let you rest *and* bring you food to eat."

Without wasting any more energy on words I reached my arm up and grasped the edge of the sink, using every last bit of my strength to pull myself into a sitting position, drawing my legs up so that he could get the door open far enough to squeeze in. I tugged the sweater down to cover myself and sighed. My head rested against the wall and I closed my eyes. Even the allure of looking at him couldn't win out over the need to just rest.

"Come on." He tugged at my feet. "Stretch your legs out so we can get your socks and pants on."

Mere seconds later he lifted me to my feet, supporting me so I could pull the sweats the rest of the way up. Making good on his promise, he carried me to my bed and settled the covers around me. My pillows never felt so good.

"I'll be right back with food. Rest."

Nobody needed to tell me twice. My eyes drifted closed, and I let the experience of the last few hours run through my head. Thanks to accepting my mother's help, we had managed to force my body to change into its wolf form. Oh!

Jerking my hand out from under the blankets, I inspected my palm. Nothing. Connecting with my wolf genes had not returned my mark. We had failed. Tears slipped down my cheeks.

"Hey, I've got-what's wrong? Are you hurt? Why are you crying?" He rushed over and sat on the edge of the bed.

Reaching up, I thrust my hand at his face. For a moment, he looked confused, then understanding dawned on his face. He grabbed my hand and ran his thumb over the bare area, bringing it up and dropping a gentle kiss where the mark should have been.

"I'm so sorry, Leah. I thought for sure that the wolf genes would heal your connection to your magic."

"It's not your fault," I whispered my response with my eyes closed.

"Do you want to eat?"

I wobbled my head against the pillow. "I just want to go to sleep. I'm sorry."

"Don't be sorry. Get some sleep. Maybe tomorrow we can go see the elders and get some advice. Or something."

"Okay."

Sleep overtook me before I heard him get up to leave the room. Even too tired to dream, the next few hours were spent in blessed blackness. When I opened my eyes again, most of the exhaustion had drained away. The body aches were still present, but greatly faded. Nothing a few Tylenol wouldn't cure.

"Hey you."

His eyes left the book in his hands and swung my way. "Well, hi there yourself. How do you feel now?"

My stomach growled, bringing us both to laughter. "Any chance that offer of breakfast in bed is still valid?"

"Absolutely. How about I make it while you shower? Do you need help down the hall?"

With very little assistance I managed to get myself into a sitting position and then out of bed. Grinning, I grabbed clean clothes and let him walk me down the hall. Today was beginning in a better head space than yesterday had ended, which made the imminent future seem a little brighter. We might be still at square one, but we'd find our way as soon as my stomach got filled up.

After a shower, I felt well enough to make it to the dining room table to eat, instead of having my food brought to me like an invalid. The bare spot on the palm of my hand continued to mock me, reminding me of the need to get my own magic back. When I got the opportunity, I wanted to see how much I could work with my mother's ring. I'd take any magic over none at all, but hers felt strange and foreign compared to my own.

Before leaving, I scribbled a note to my mother, who still slept, and left it on the dining room table. Stopping by the pantry, I also grabbed a few crackers to continue mending the fence with my two little friends. They were nowhere to be seen this morning, but the offering I'd left earlier was gone.

As we walked down the trail, Isaiah looked at me, studying my face. "What made you decide to accept your mother's help? You were so against it at first."

My lips pursed as I exhaled loudly through them, sputtering as I did so. "I had no other choice. As soon as you left, she was waiting to talk to me. She apologized again, and offered me not only help in pulling my wolf forward, by using the same spell I used on you, but a token to share some of her own magic as well."

I held my hand out so he could see the ring, the only item that had not disappeared with my shift to wolf and back. He pulled it closer to get a good look, then let go. His face held little to give away his feelings.

"I realized refusing her would be selfish. No matter how hard you and I worked, we couldn't make my wolf appear. If she could force it, and possibly bring my mark back, saying no would be like cutting off my nose to spite my face. I'd fail because I was prideful, and it would be nobody's fault but my own. Letting the spirit win because I was angry would just make me a childish brat."

"Well, I'm glad you accepted her help, and I really am sorry it didn't return your mark. How does it feel to have her magic to use?"

"I'm not sure yet. Strange, definitely. It is very different from before. It feels foreign and complicated, not as natural as when I began using my own. I need to take some time today and work with it to see what capabilities I have and don't have. It's no good to me at all if I don't know how to work it."

Reaching out, I tugged him to a stop for a second at the fork in the trail. Left would lead us to the pack village, the right would take us toward the temple. An idea was forming in my head.

"Do you mind making a detour to the temple? I

want to try something."

"Are you sure that's a good idea?"

"Why not? It's empty now. She's gone. According to what I've learned so far, the temple was once a place for the worship of the goddess connected to the sanctuary. I'd like to go back and clean it up a little, perform a ritual to cleanse it, and try to restore some of the sanctity of it. I feel the need to try and mend fences with her, to show her I am worthy of the mark and perhaps she will change her mind and return it to me."

He didn't speak at first, mulling over my explanation. Then, without a word, he turned to the right and began following the trail toward the temple. We continued on in silence until we reached the crumbling wall that marked the perimeter of the temple grounds.

Second thoughts made me pause. As much as I believed my theory was correct that she had gone far from this place, we had nothing to keep her out. Unless the banishment prevented her from returning. It hadn't occurred to me to ask my mom about it. Banishment, however, by definition, prevented one's return to a place. We wouldn't know until we tried.

"Ready?"

At my nod, he took my hand and helped me over the piles of unsteady stones. With both feet on the temple grounds, I stood and reached out with my senses, looking for any indication it might not be safe. All I could feel was quiet. No dark presence or heavy air surrounded the building, as it had for my first few visits.

"It feels clear to me. Let's go."

We made our way inside, crossing the threshold with tentative footsteps. Asking the first thing of my mother's magic, I attempted to use the spell that would give me an orb of light. The magic gave me what I asked for, although different. This orb was orange-ish in color, not the pure white of my original one. It bathed the room in a glow that reminded me of firelight, but at least we could see.

"What do you want me to do?" This trip inside was his first that had not been prompted by a panicked situation, and his eyes roamed the space, taking in the details.

"Will you start by standing up as many of the

columns and pedestals that you can? I know some are broken, and I will try a spell to repair them, but I'd like to get as many of the statues returned to their rightful place as possible. While you do that I am going to try and remember how the altar was laid out so I can begin setting it to rights again."

Ignoring the fact that my last good study of the altar had been with my aunt's body laying at the foot of it, I began returning the bowls, crystals and candles to their previous resting places. We worked in silence, Isaiah only occasionally asking me what I thought about something. Surveying the room, I made a mental list of the things I wanted to bring back on my next trip to help restore the space.

Isaiah stood at the back of the room while I knelt on the stair in front of the altar. Bowing my head, I murmured to the goddess that I hoped truly existed. I made it as heartfelt and formal as I knew how.

"Forgive me, for I have not yet read your name or know what to call you. I know the temple has not been returned to its former glory, but I will do my best to continue working toward restoring it. Please forgive my mistake in believing the tricks of the evil spirit. Forgive me that she is my ancestor. I am trying so hard to make things right. Even if you do not see fit to return my mark, please guide me to help those who live here under your care. I am thankful I had the mark and the magic you granted to begin with, and I will work hard to earn it back."

Standing, I turned and joined Isaiah at the edge of the entrance hall. He took my hand and gave it a squeeze.

"I think you had an excellent idea. It looks pretty good in here."

"I need to do more, but at least I'm not leaving it the disaster that it was."

We made our way to the wolves' village, making inconsequential small talk on the way. I wanted to ask him about my wolf form, but didn't get the courage to do so. When we reached the settlement, my thoughts immediately turned to the situation that needed to be dealt with there.

CHAPTER FIVE

"Where the hell have you been?" Sam, Isaiah's beta, snarled at us the second we emerged from the tree line. He stalked up to us, hands on his hips, cheeks bright red.

"Excuse me? Know your place, Sam," Isaiah snarled right back, refusing to allow any of the pack to speak to him that way.

"While you were off playing house with your little witchy girlfriend there, the evil spirit was terrorizing our pack!" Sam glanced at me with a sneer as he said it.

"And why wasn't I called? I've been available this entire time, and absolutely *nobody* reached out to me and apprised me of the situation."

"What?" Sam's tone lost some of its venom. "Aden said he'd been calling for you repeatedly and you refused to answer him."

Isaiah slowly shook his head. "He didn't reach out to me once. Why didn't you try?"

Sam stood down, turning his gaze to the center wolves and humans milling around the town's square. He shifted his weight from foot to foot, watching. Isaiah didn't wait for a response before jumping on him.

"And don't you ever refer to Leah that way again. If it weren't for her, you'd still be standing in front of me on four legs instead of two. Is that clear? She deserves your utmost respect for what she sacrificed to help us."

Sam turned to me, mouth down-turned. "I'm sorry. I was out of line, and I let my frustrations override my judgment. We all appreciate what you did for us, and I am sorry it cost you your magic to do it."

"Don't worry about it. I have a habit of saying things I don't mean when I'm emotional, too. Not one of my better traits, but there you have it." I shrugged at him. "And I would do it all over again in a heartbeat. We will try to get my magic back."

Isaiah let us have our little moment before interrupting. "Now, what's this about the spirit being here in the village? The wards should have kept her out, no problem. Especially since she is weakened from Leah's mother banishing her."

"Well, to be fair, we didn't actually *see* her. Strange things kept happening, and wherever they went on these blue lights kept flickering, just like at the temple and the stream."

"Hm. I wonder why Aden lied about attempting to reach me." Puzzlement dominated Isaiah's expression.

"I might have the answer to that." Sam looked sheepish, redirecting his gaze to the ground and stuffing his hands in his pockets.

"Well?"

My eyes bounced between the two of them,

curious about what made Sam so embarrassed. He looked everywhere but at Isaiah or I. Isaiah, on the other hand, stared right at him as he waited for a response.

"So..." He took a deep breath. "Aden made a big deal, very quietly mind you, about how it was entirely possible that Leah was in the perfect position to be responsible for the whole bit." His words rushed out once they got started. "He even suggested that maybe she only pretended to lose her magic so that nobody would suspect her when the shit started hitting the fan again. Leah, I'm so sorry. I want you to know that most of the pack didn't believe him."

My mouth gaped as I stared at him. The pack thought that lowly of me? Even after the amount of time I spent attempting to forge friendships with them? My heart sank to my toes as the blood rose in my cheeks.

"What?" Isaiah roared the single word, garnering the attention of everyone in the area. His eyes narrowed as they focused on Sam. "Get him, and bring him to the meeting hall *right now,* whether he wants to come or not."

Without waiting for an answer, he grabbed my hand and strode off in the direction of the town center. Panting hard within a few steps, I tugged on his hand to slow him down.

"Remember, my legs are about half as long as yours, and I had a rough day yesterday."

He met my eyes sheepishly. "I'm sorry. I just got so pissed off I didn't stop to think about you having to keep up."

His pace matched mine as we walked the rest of the way to a building near the center of the town square. He pushed the unlocked door open and led me over the uneven wooden threshold. The room itself had a lectern at the front and numerous wood benches, resembling church pews, filled a sizable portion of the main room.

He veered around the edge of the room to a door on the left side of the room, unlocking it with a key from the set in his pocket. "Come on in." He stepped aside and ushered me through first.

The room itself was unremarkable, holding a plain desk, a set of bookshelves, and a pair of comfortable-looking chairs. He gestured for me to sit on one of the chairs while perching on the edge of the desk, his legs stretched out in front of him. His strong hands gripped the edge of the desk, white knuckles the only physical indication of his irritation.

"Is this your office?" For some reason, it surprised me that a pack of werewolves had an office building.

"It's technically the office of whoever is the reigning alpha, so currently, yes, it is mine. I don't really use it all that much, though. No need yet since things just started getting back to normal."

"I'm not sure that normal is the word you want to use to describe what is going on right now. I'd prefer to think that our current situation is abnormal and will someday return to a more reasonable flow of daily life." My nose wrinkled at the thought that the rest of my life would be this chaotic.

He grunted. Before he could respond, we heard the front door opening and some scuffling as at least two people walked in. Isaiah could probably make out the barely grumbled words, but I had no idea, other than the tone of them came across as less than pleased.

Sam entered, escorting a short blond man with a scowl on his face. What he lacked in height he made up for in muscles. This guy was built like a miniature Mack truck. I could see a third man waiting just outside the doorway, who made no move to enter behind the other two.

Sam shoved the man, who I now assumed to be Aden, into the room ahead of him and then stood blocking the doorway, and my view of the man remaining outside. My attention returned to Aden, wondering what I had done to make him hate me so. We'd never even been introduced.

"I heard there was some trouble while I was gone." Isaiah issued the statement easily, no emotion in his tone.

Aden swallowed, then looked at me briefly, before turning around to glance at Sam, who kept a neutral expression on his face. "A little. Nothing we couldn't handle."

"Well, that's good. I'd hate to think that I couldn't even leave the village for a few hours with some of my most trusted men in charge. Anything else you'd like to report?"

Aden shifted from foot to foot. He couldn't seem to decide what to do with his arms, and they moved in a continuous cycle from hanging at his sides, to crossed in front of him, to clasped behind his back.

Glancing at Isaiah, I raised my eyebrows, looking for permission to interject. He nodded slightly, and I turned my focus on Aden. He refused to meet my eyes.

"What, exactly, is your problem with me?"

"I don't know what you mean." His shifty green eyes looked to Isaiah for guidance, but he stood perfectly still, not offering any hint of how he expected this to play out.

I took two steps in his direction, stopping just short of being chest to chest with him, my head tilted up slightly. His eyes darted all over the room, landing everywhere but my face. Without moving another muscle, I demanded that he look at me.

"You owe me that much, at least, after the rumors you tried to spread about me."

Aden's head whipped around, pegging Sam with a glare. Sam didn't so much as flinch, meeting Aden's gaze head on. After spending tense seconds either trying to read Sam's face or intimidate him, he turned back to me.

"I don't owe you anything."

Very deliberately, I reached out and trailed my index finger down his bare forearm. He flinched at the contact.

"Except this, maybe? Had I not chosen to break the curse, your human skin wouldn't even exist right now. What if I elected to take it back?"

His breathing elevated as his eyes narrowed. "You can't. I thought you lost your magic?"

"Then why would you tell everyone I was only pretending to be without my magic? Hm? You can't have it both ways, my friend."

As I reached out to touch him again, he slapped my hand away and I let out a little laugh. Both Isaiah and Sam growled instantly, although neither of them moved a muscle. They were leaving me to play the lead role in this charade.

Instead of touching him, I leaned in until our faces were centimeters apart and whispered. "Never underestimate me, Aden. My magic may be temporarily unreachable, but I come from a long line of witches. Ones who are more than willing to share their power with me until mine returns."

Leaning back to give myself a little room, I rubbed my hands together, calling forth a tiny bit of electricity. The arcing power sprang to life between my hands. Extending my arms, I held it out for him to see. He flinched, then scowled.

"I can be your best friend, or your worst enemy. I sacrificed what I did for this pack because I believed it was my duty, and I believed that all were worthy. Do not make me regret it. It would be most unpleasant if I had to change you back."

"Try it," the quaver in his voice belied the macho image he tried desperately to project.

I stepped back out of his bubble nonchalantly, inspecting my fingernails. "Nah. Don't really want to be bothered at the moment. But I'd think long and hard about my choices in the future, if I were you. Don't be making rash decisions based on nothing. That's how people get hurt. And we wouldn't want that."

Sinking back into the chair, I proceeded to ignore him as if he'd disappeared.

"Are you going to let her talk to me like that?" He turned to Sam. "Did you see that? She threatened me!"

Sam scoffed. "Threatened you? She's barely five feet tall. Surely you aren't afraid of a tiny, practically magic-less little witch, are you?"

I had to bite my cheek to keep from noticeably smirking at the tone in Sam's voice. Isaiah managed to maintain his expression, too.

"Look, Aden," Isaiah began, "this is the thing. If you have a problem with me, come to me and discuss it. Spreading rumors about the only person who was able to help this pack isn't the way to go about things."

"Like you'd listen? You're barely ever here anyways, always out with her. At her house, walking in the woods. This pack needs a *real* alpha, not a lovesick teenager."

"I appreciate that you've brought that to my attention, and I shall meet with you again to discuss it more. You're free to go."

Aden turned on his heel and stalked out the door, pushing by Sam as he went. Sam came in and took the chair across from me. Isaiah met his eyes.

"Is Aden the only one who feels that way?"

Sam hesitated before shaking his head. "No, unfortunately. There is a small group who agrees with him, and he is doing his best to convince others as well." He paused, then glanced at me before meeting Isaiah's eyes and continuing. "You are gone an awful lot."

Isaiah sighed. "I am. Maybe too much. I need to spend more time here until I can reign in some of the dissent. Be more present."

"I didn't mean to take you away from your duties," I began.

"You didn't. I came this time because I knew you needed me, but I will need to spend more time here. Maybe I should walk you back and ask the elders those questions myself. I will let you know what they say?"

Sam stood. "I'll leave you to it and keep an eye on things until you get back."

"Thanks, Sam." He watched as Sam made his way out the door, remaining silent until we heard the front doors thud shut behind him. "I'm sorry about all this."

"Don't be. I get it. Let's head back so you can return and take care of your obligations."

More people had gathered in the square, perhaps just being nosy. We passed them all, offering a wave or friendly hello. Most of them responded in kind. A few snubbed me, but not many. Those who did were grudgingly respectful of Isaiah.

As we walked, we talked of how the pack worked, and how he became alpha.

"Why did you kill him? Did you always want to be alpha?"

Isaiah let out a harsh laugh. "Never. But he was not a good dude. Many of the elders believe he had some secret dealing with the outsiders who found their way to the reserve while your grandmother was still powerful. We could never prove it, but many of the suspicious things stopped once he was dead. I just stepped into the role because I was the one to take him out. I believe I can do good for this pack and the sanctuary."

"I think you can too." I reached out and grabbed his hand. "I'll help if I can. But maybe it's best if I lay low at the house for a few days, and let you focus on what needs to be done there?"

"As much as I hate to admit, I think it would be good to do that. I will continue to convince them you are our best hope for eliminating the evil spirit entirely."

"For now, I need to focus on getting my magic back. Without it, I have no hope of beating her."

It was his turn to squeeze my hand. "We'll figure it out. Somehow."

Just before the curve in the trail that led to the clearing, he tugged me to a stop, turning me to face him. My stomach fluttered at the look in his eyes. He held both of my hands between both of his, encircling them completely.

"Thank you. For all you've done so far. In spite of the circumstances, I am so glad you're here."

My heart melted a little. "Me too. We'll get through this."

"And when we do, will you stay? Here at the sanctuary?"

"Maybe. I'm certainly thinking about it."

"Good. I'd like you to." He leaned in a brushed a

gentle kiss across my forehead. "Get inside. I'll watch you until you're in the door."

I rounded the curve, crossed the clearing and slipped inside, coming face to face with my mother, who sat at the table.

"Leah, we need to have a talk."

CHAPTER SIX

The tone in her voice set my teeth on edge before any other words made it out of her mouth. Biting back a sigh, I latched the back door and threw the dead bolt, buying a few precious seconds before facing her again. After the showdown with Aden, I wasn't really in the mood to take anyone else's shit, even my mother's.

"What about?"

"Your plans. What you intend to do now." She met my stare with a stubborn gaze.

"You know what my intentions are. I am not leaving this sanctuary until my crescent mark returns and my magic has been restored. Once that happens, I am going to do my damnedest to make sure the spirit of your mother can't continue to roam the Earth wreaking havoc. It's pretty straightforward."

Before she could answer, I stood up, moving into the kitchen to put on a kettle of water for tea. Grabbing a mug out of the cupboard, I held it in her direction, silently inquiring if she wanted one. She nodded in acceptance. The conversation didn't resume until I returned to the table with our cups and all the accompaniments for our tea.

"I understand why you want to do this-" she began.

"Do you, though? Do you really understand? Because you were the one who ran away and abandoned this sanctuary, the wolves, and your own sister. I'm not sure you have a real good understanding of the concept of responsibility to others."

She flinched, but didn't turn away. "My only responsibilities in this world are to myself and you, to my daughter."

"I appreciate the help you offered. I really do. But that doesn't mean I am going to abandon the sanctuary just because you want to go home."

"Leah. I don't think you understand what you are up against. She almost killed you once. She *did kill* Aimee. You are not powerful enough to best her."

"And whose fault is that, hmm?" I set my tea down on the tabletop a little harder than I'd intended, and the handle cracked off in my hand.

For a brief moment, my entire focus was on that piece of porcelain resting in my palm. Curving my hand, I rolled it from side to side against my skin. The off white of the interior stood out starkly against the painted blue of the outer layer. My thumb ran over the smooth enamel outside and paused at the jagged edge separating it from the uneven inside.

"I already apologized for that Leah Catherine. Stop throwing my mistakes back in my face. I am doing everything possible to make up for my choices. I thought I was doing what was best for you! I wanted to protect you!"

"Because you stole my ability to protect myself!"

A tear slipped down her cheek. She shook her head back and forth, chewing on her bottom lip. Her hands trembled so hard that her tea cup rattled against the tabletop.

"I know," she whispered. "Which is why I am so desperate to get you away from here, because I can't protect you either."

Her eyes never left the tabletop as I watched her. My anger warred with my empathy. In the end, I decided not to continue the conversation, for fear I would say something I regretted.

"I'm going to bed. I'm exhausted and I need the rest. Goodnight."

Her voice followed me as I walked down the hall. "I love you, Leah."

"I know, Mom. I love you too."

The bedroom door latch clicked, and I stood for a minute with my hand still on the knob, taking in the space. The furnishings hadn't changed since I was young, and I remembered shopping with my aunt for the pieces to go in "my" room. We spent an entire day in town, driving from store to store, testing mattresses and checking dresser drawers. We'd settled on this set because it was off-white, instead of plain, brown wood.

At the time, the room made me feel like such a grownup with a full size bed instead of a twin, and all the matching pieces. I walked over to one of the two matching nightstands and pulled open the drawer, which I hadn't done since arriving. The detritus of a teenage girl's life littered the bottom.

A small notepad lay next to a couple of glitter pens. Numerous hairbands, which, funnily enough, I could never find when I actually wanted to put my hair up. I reached out and picked up the well-loved copy of my absolute favorite book. The spine was cracked and the cover bent, the pages dog-eared and worn.

Wizard's First Rule, by Terry Goodkind. The irony that I had loved reading about wizards and magic to escape from the real world, while all that the sanctuary was lying hidden right beneath my nose, was not lost on me. The rest of the series sat on the bookcase in the library, and I had read it a hundred times over.

Changing into some sweats, I climbed into the

bed and propped the pillows behind me. As I opened it to the first page, a photo that I always used as a bookmark fell from between the pages. Aimee and I, sound asleep during a nap on the couch downstairs, both of us had books in our laps. Mine happened to be the fourth book from the series I was about to begin again. I couldn't see hers and didn't remember what she'd been reading after all this time. My mom took the photo when she came to pick me up one time.

Tears rushed my eyes, spilling over before I realized they were coming. It bothered me that I didn't remember the book resting on her legs. These pictures were priceless now. I might have all these material things around me to remind me of her, but they weren't enough. They didn't show you her shining eyes, or let you hear her joyous laughter. And none of the magic at her disposal had been able to save her life.

The tears impeded my ability to read, and instead of trying, I curled up on my side, holding the book to me with the photo returned safely between the pages. With the covers tugged over my head, I begged for the universe, or the sanctuary goddess, or whatever god there was to listen, to restore my mark and give my magic back to me. I pleaded and bargained, promising not to be so foolish with it the next time.

At some point, the need for sleep overtook me and I dozed fitfully. After jerking awake for what felt like the hundredth time, I poked my head out of the blankets. Bleary-eyed and with a pounding headache, I squinted at the clock on the nightstand. I'd made it until six a.m.

Desperate for relief, I hobbled to the kitchen and turned the coffee pot on before heading to the bathroom for a shower and something to relieve the aching in my skull. The hot water and steam did little for me, although the rinsing with cool water after soothed my gritty eyes.

Our cups from the night before remained on the table, the broken handle sitting jauntily beside the cup it had been split from. The dishwasher hadn't been emptied, and I pulled a cup from the rack. My fear of breaking the unicorn mug meant I left it in the cupboard, moved to the back so it couldn't be knocked out by accident. A regular mug would have to do.

Ensconced on one of the porch chairs, I sipped my coffee while I waited for the world around me to wake up. The sky lightened and birds chirped in the distance. Once the mug no longer held what I deemed to be magic bean water, I set it on the small table. It was then that I noticed the small pile of pine cones, some crystalline stones and a small metal object. Round, like a coin, it had more depth to it than one. A strange symbol had been etched on either side. Curious, I slipped it into my pocket. I'd check the books for information later.

A knocking at the front door echoed through the house, startling me. Since I hadn't heard a car pull up, whoever it was must have found their way here on foot. Rushing through the house, I slid to a stop before the large wooden door, barely avoiding crashing into it.

Throwing the dead bolt, I pulled it open. Two dark-haired men in uniform stood before me.

"Can I help you?"

"We are from the county police department. We'd like to discuss the release of your Aunt Aimee's body. May we come in?"

"Yes, of course." I stood aside, motioning them through the door. Distracted by their deep red lips, I didn't hear my mother come barreling down the hallway.

"Absolutely NOT."

Shocked at her rudeness, all I could do was stare. She herded the strangers right back out onto the porch. They looked sideways at each other but didn't argue.

She elbowed me to the side and pulled the front door mostly closed. "Thank you, but you didn't need to come all the way out here. One of your colleagues already made arrangements by phone."

The two of them looked surprised by that information, but again, didn't argue. Both of them nodded politely at her and turned to walk towards the car I had been certain wouldn't be there.

"Sorry to bother you, ma'am."

With their last sentence, both of them got in the car and shut the doors. The engine turned over, and they backed out, turning down the gravel drive. My mother watched until they were out of sight. Then she slammed the door shut and locked it, turning to me.

"Never, *ever*, invite a stranger into you home. It gives them access to you in the future."

"What?" Her tone surprised me. For someone who invited everyone from the mailman to the lawn service guy into our home, this sudden change of heart seemed strange.

"Just don't, okay? Not here, in this place. I'm going to take a shower."

My gaze followed her as she turned around and went right back down the hall with no further conversation. Restless after the encounter, I decided to take a walk. Aside from the few trails we regularly took, I hadn't been in much of the forest. Crossing the imaginary line between the house and the forest brought me a modicum of peace. I let my feet find their way while I worked through my situation with my mother.

She seemed to get more and more strange with each passing day. It drove me crazy that she thought I should just up and leave the sanctuary without any thought for those who lived here. Like she didn't care about avenging her own sister's death. Or protecting everyone else in the world from the spirit of her crazy ass mother. How could a person be so selfish?

I loved her, I really did. And I didn't in any way believe that she had made her choices with the intention of making things hard for me in my future. But that didn't negate the fact that they had done just that.

The garnet ring still rested on my hand. Holding it between my fingers, I lifted it up and peered at it from different angles. If one of the tiny rays of sunlight filtering through the trees above managed to catch the stone, it looked as if it danced with flames from within.

At the base of a large tree, I stopped, settling down to meditate. My mother's magic still felt foreign and strange, and I'd taken very little time to work with it. Putting the lessons from the books in the attic to good use, I took my socks and shoes off, digging my toes into the dirt in an attempt to be closer to the sanctuary itself.

With the ring clutched in my hand, I closed my eyes and broadened my senses, attempting to take in the power around me with the help of my mother's gift. The experiment was meant to see whether I still harbored the ability for gathering magic from the world around me, even if I could not produce it on my own.

It hovered right outside of my awareness, like trying to get hold of a slippery beach ball bouncing in the waves. My fingers would just brush the edges of it before it skittered out of reach. No amount of effort would coax it closer. While it didn't seem to actively shun me, it didn't welcome me either.

Giving up momentarily, I leaned my head back against the bark of the tree and left my eyes closed, relying on my other senses to take in the forest around me. The ring returned to its place on my hand. Instead of trying to capture the essence, I opened myself and invited it to come to me.

Tugging on my hair pulled me from my reverie. Realizing I must have dozed off, I sat up, eliciting a squeak from behind me. After craning my neck to set a better look, my gaze landed on the pair of chipmunks from the tree near the house.

"Well, hello there. I didn't bring any snacks with me this time."

They took turns chattering at me, running up and down the tree trunk and out onto the branches. One of them returned with a pine cone and dropped it at my side. The other disappeared from view before returning with a gorgeous rock, which I tentatively identified as a banded agate. It must have come from the stream bed to be so smoothly polished.

"Thank you so much! I love them both."

I turned the agate over in my hands, marveling at its colors. Banded agates, if I remembered correctly, are stones of protection and used to restore bodily energy or ease your mind when in stressful situations. I'd say I qualified as needing all of the above.

Getting to my feet, I slipped both in the pocket of my jeans, where they'd be less likely to fall out and get lost. My little friends climbed back up and perched on the lowest branch.

"I owe you guys some cookies when I get home. Deal? But I need to head out now."

Their chattering floated on the breeze as I moved back down the trail. Reaching the fork where I could either head home or toward the pack village, something encouraged me not to head home just yet.

Trusting it, I moved down the trail leading toward Isaiah and the pack.

As I got closer to the village, I could feel a disturbance in the energy that usually wasn't there. Without my magic, I couldn't accurately sense what it was, but I felt it. As I crossed the border, I could see the pack milling about the square anxiously. So far, I had a hard time identifying everyone when they were in wolf form, but I could recognize them as humans easily. Isaiah was nowhere in sight.

Thankfully, Aden didn't seem to be in the vicinity. Shelby, one of the women I had begun to form a friendship with, stood at the edge of the grass with two others that I hadn't met yet. Hesitantly, I walked up to them.

As soon as she caught sight of me, Shelby squealed and threw her arms around me. "Leah! I am so glad to see you. This is Amber and Evie. Girls, this is Leah."

We exchanged pleasantries for a minute before I was able to ask what everyone seemed so worked up about.

"A stranger appeared today. He was found

wandering the land near the temple and brought back here. He says he came from the North Eastern pack. He's fairly young, with dark hair and green eyes. Do you know him?"

CHAPTER SEVEN

"I don't know anyone from the other pack. I didn't even know they existed until a few days ago. Of course, I didn't know all of you existed until recently, either."

Someone from the other pack? My curiosity was piqued. At one time I'd asked Isaiah if we could go there, and now one of their members suddenly appeared over here. Unable to decide if it seemed suspicious, I scanned the crowd for Isaiah. Not seeing him, I reached out via our private path and asked him what he wanted me to do since I was here.

"Come on over to the alpha's office. You should probably meet him."

I let Shelby know I would be sure to see her before I left, and said my goodbyes to the other two. "It was nice to meet you."

It felt strange to cross the crowded square without Isaiah at my side. Numerous pairs of eyes bored into my back as I passed. Making sure to smile and wave at those I knew, I made it to the office building with minimal discomfort.

Until I walked up to the covered porch area. Lounging against the side of the building was Aden, arms crossed and a scowl on his face. "Back again so soon, are you?"

Knowing I needed to take a stand with him and reinforce our boundaries after the last meeting, I stood my ground. Quirking my lips up in a smug smile, I shrugged with one shoulder. "Why Aden. It's *so* good to see you again. And so soon. How are you?"

He snarled in response. "You may think you've got everyone here charmed, but I know the truth. You won't get away with what you're doing, and if you don't leave Isaiah out of it, he will lose everything. And I mean *everything*."

"Oh? And what, precisely, am I doing? I have done nothing but try to help this pack."

"That's what you want everyone to think. I'm not stupid, and there are plenty of other members of this pack who aren't either."

As he spoke, he pushed himself off the wall and took two steps forward. Knowing his wolf would smell my fear if I let it get hold, I didn't move, allowing him to get right up in my space without flinching. Barely taller than me by a couple of inches, we stood nose to nose, gazes clashing. I raised my eyebrows and tilted my head just slightly.

"It sounds to me like you guys might actually be the stupid ones."

"You won't always have someone around to protect you, little miss Leah."

"Ah, you're right Aden. And do you know why that doesn't worry me? I can protect myself. I thought I had proven that already, but maybe you need a reminder?"

He backed a couple of inches away at my

statement, thrown off by the fact that he hadn't been able to scare me. "Watch yourself. There are plenty around here that you don't even know exist who aren't happy with your meddling. And if you push the issue too far, they will have no problem putting an immediate stop to it."

He spun on his heel and stomped off, gathering more attention from those gathered around the area. Curious eyes tracked his progress. Gazes swung from his retreating form to me, standing as casually as I could muster, and back to him again. Many of those nearby had undoubtedly heard our exchange, thanks to their fantastic hearing. I couldn't help but wonder how many of them thought just like him. Waiting until he was out of sight across the square, I let out a sigh and turned to go into the building.

Sam was standing just inside the door. "Hey, Leah. I heard your exchange with Aden, but didn't want to butt in since you sounded like you had it handled. He needs to see that you can stand up for yourself."

"Hey Sam. Thanks. He creeps me out, but I'll be damned if I'm going to let him bully me. Asshole."

"You did great, if that's any help for your confidence. What brings you this way? Did you know we have a visitor?"

"I just found out from Shelby when I got here. Any news?"

"Isaiah will fill you in. He's expecting you. Go on into the office," he gestured toward the closed door.

Before I could know, the door opened, and Isaiah stepped out. "Sam, would you sit with him for a minute, please?"

"Sure thing." Sam stepped in and closed the door behind him as Isaiah moved over to stand next to me.

"It's the weirdest thing," he began, not speaking the words out loud. "He seemed to come out of nowhere. I didn't feel him cross into our territory at all, then all of a sudden I could feel his presence near the temple."

"Like he just dropped out of the sky?" That seemed unlikely to me.

"Exactly, and he was pretty severely injured, although he couldn't tell us what happened. He claimed he didn't remember traveling or getting injured. He just came to sitting against the wall at the outside of the temple yard. He said he'd barely been conscious for a few minutes when we got to him."

"Do you believe him?"

"I'm not sure. He hasn't been willing to say much else." Isaiah spoke the words slowly, and his indecision washed through me.

"Can I meet him?"

"Yeah, I think that would be a good idea. If anything, he may open up to you more than he will to me. And we should take the opportunity to gather as much information as we can about him and the pack on the other side of the sanctuary. It's been years since we had any contact with them."

We headed back toward the closed door, and I could hear the low murmur of voices on the other side, but not make out the words. Isaiah pushed the door open, and Sam nodded at us before exiting and shutting the door behind him.

The young man sat in one of the chairs in front of the desk, appearing to be calm, at least for the moment. He met my eyes as I perched on the edge of the desk in front of him, and the first thing that struck me was the tiniest shoots of blue woven through them, despite the fact that they were a stark emerald green.

He slouched against the back of the chair, leaning heavily against the arm on his left side. His hair stuck out in disarray and his expression made me worry about his health. Fair skin stretched over sharp cheekbones. Purplish-blue stains filled the depressions below his green eyes. The skin on his lips cracked and peeled at the corners of his mouth. Aside from being a little on the skinny side, I didn't note any other physical issues.

"Hey. I'm Leah. What's your name?"

"Nice to meet you, Leah. I'm Aaron." His voice was low pitched and strained, but not difficult to understand.

"Are you feeling okay?" I wanted to hear his own assessment and see if he could tell me anything else about how he got here.

"Oh yeah, or I will be. I'm healing pretty quickly."

"How did you get injured?"

He gave a little laugh. "They think that if they have you ask the questions that my answers will change?"

"I'm sorry?"

"They've already asked me, and I already answered. I don't know how I got injured. I'm not sure how I ended up where they found me. Trust me, if I had more to tell, I would have told it."

I bit my lip for a second before asking another question. A knock at the door came before I could decide which direction to take with my queries next. Sam and two of the elders stood on the other side when Isaiah opened it.

I scooted away from the middle of the action and off toward a corner where I would be out of the way, but still present, to hear what this Aaron had to say. Isaiah made introductions, and the elders began asking their questions. The newcomer answered them quickly, if succinctly, and without hesitation. Based on my limited body language observation skills, nothing they asked of him appeared to make him uncomfortable.

"And what brought you into our territory? None of our pack has ever seen you before."

Aaron took a deep breath. "So, that's the strange part. I was sitting up on one of the mountain ledges, where I go hiking often. A strange electricity was in the air. Looking out this way, an unnatural cloud seemed to be forming. The lightning in it sparked bright blue, instead of the regular white. For a while I just sat and watched it, and it seemed to be growing."

Aaron reached up and pushed his hair back, then rubbed his face. He pinched the bridge of his nose, as if trying to ward off a headache. His brow furrowed as he continued his story.

"I decided I should go tell my alpha, in case it was something we needed to be on guard for. I started heading back down the trail toward home when I got an intense headache. I kept walking, but the dizziness made it slow going, and I started seeing double, which made it even harder to make my way down the trail without falling. Even shifting didn't help."

His eyes took on a faraway look, and he bit his cheek as he looked for the words he wanted to use. He hesitated for the first time during the entire interrogation. To me, it seemed more like he was trying to remember the sequence of events rather than avoid answering.

"After that, everything gets real fuzzy. I vaguely

recall crossing a stream at some point, and then being surprised my pants were all wet. But I can't tell you how I got there or how I got across. After that, the next thing that is clear is that I was sitting on the ground leaning up against a rock wall that was falling down. I tried to stand up and see where I was, but I was too injured. I needed to wait for my body to heal. You guys found me before that could happen. And here I am."

The elders looked sideways at each other, then over at Isaiah. I knew they were conferring in private before any of them made another decision. I couldn't help wonder what they were saying, and hope Isaiah would be willing to fill me in.

Their conversation took long enough that Aaron started to look uncomfortable and shifted in his seat. "Is there a bathroom I can use?"

Isaiah nodded Sam's way, who left his place against the wall. "Sure, right this way."

Once the door closed behind him, the conversation resumed, now in whispers so that I could follow along. The three leading wolves talked about Aaron's story. They didn't seem to know what to make of it.

"The easiest lies to keep to are the ones that are the simplest," pointed out one of the elders, whose name was William.

"What reason could the other pack possibly have to send a spy here?" the other elder, Jerry, posed the question.

Isaiah answered him with hesitation. "We don't know, but there is still much we do not know. We'll need more information before we can settle on any course of permanent action. For now, we need to decide what we are going to do with him. Do we let him stay temporarily? He doesn't appear to be an immediate threat."

"Well, I wouldn't be comfortable sending him back out into our territory without an escort, so I don't see why he can't stay for a few days," William made his statement, and Jerry agreed with him. "

"There are more than enough of us to keep an eye on him."

Having settled on a short-term plan, the three of them discussed whether they needed to ask any more questions of him. Before they settled on any, the door swung open and Aaron and Sam returned.

Isaiah turned toward Aaron. "We're willing to put you up for a few days until you are completely healed. No funny business, though, and we will know if you try anything."

"I wouldn't dream of it. No matter what you think, I did not come here with evil intentions."

The word evil caught my attention. Why had he chosen that particular word, when plenty of others would have done? My eyes met his, searching for clues. I saw none.

As Sam prepared to lead him out the door, I called out. "Hey Aaron?"

He stopped and turned to face me, and on the door frame for support. "Yeah?"

"What's your alpha's name?"

"Oh, his name is Rick."

CHAPTER EIGHT

He turned and followed Sam out the door without waiting to see if I had anything else to say. Both elders left right behind them, closing the door on their way out. The look on my face must have given away my feelings of shock and surprise, because Isaiah walked over and laid his hand on my arm. He gave it a squeeze.

"You don't think..." he began.

"I don't believe in coincidences. It has to be him. Doesn't it?"

"Let's not get your hopes up just yet. Tomorrow, we can ask a few more questions and see what he says. Something about this whole situation just seems fishy to me."

Anticipation flooded me. Could the Rick of the other pack really be my Aunt Aimee's long-lost husband? My uncle? If he had been here this whole time, wouldn't she have been able to find him? Either with her magic or by searching the property, it would have taken immense effort to hide from her when she looked so diligently for him. And if the two were one and the same, why?

"It does feel off somehow, doesn't it? I can't put my finger on it, but the whole thing doesn't add up. I didn't get the feeling he was lying to us, or even trying to hide the truth, and yet something tells me that there is more to the story. Somehow, we are missing a major piece of the puzzle."

"I heard you had a run-in with Aden on your way in. You okay?"

"Oh, I'm fine. He's just trying to bully me. I refuse to let him. I'm not his favorite person, that's for sure."

"Let me know if he really starts to give you trouble. I'll intervene."

"I think it's best if you don't, not unless it becomes really necessary. That will just make him feel even more animosity towards me and make him question whether I really can take care of myself. So far, he's just being a nuisance. He's not hurting me."

"If you're sure..." He let the words trail off, his tone relaying that he didn't quite agree with my take on it, but was going to let me handle it my way for now. "I want to go do some scouting around the temple and back toward the stream. Will you wait here, or do you want to head back to your house?"

I snorted. "I'd love to avoid my mother for a bit, so if it's not too much trouble, I'd prefer to hang out around here."

"What happened now? You guys were just getting along fine." Exasperation bled through his attempt to be neutral.

My temper bristled at his judgmental tone, but I tried not to let it show. "She tried telling me I need to pack up and leave the sanctuary. After trying to assure me she would do everything she could to help me." My sarcasm colored the words as I repeated her sentences. "Blah blah blah, she's too weak to protect me from her mother. I should go far away so she doesn't come after me, yada yada yada. As if that crazy woman wouldn't come after me as soon as she had enough power to leave the sanctuary?"

"I have to admit I believed her when she said she would help you from here on out, so that surprises me a little. But it is what it is. Maybe she'll come around for real next time." He rolled his eyes, signaling he thought the idea unlikely. "At any rate, of course, you're welcome to stay. Maybe go hang out with Shelby?"

"Actually, I was thinking I'd go talk to Aaron. Maybe he will feel less threatened and open up to me if it's just the two of us."

Isaiah pursed his lips, leaving me to wonder for a second if he was going to tell me what a terrible idea it was, but he surprised me. "I think that might be smart. We've given him a guest cottage right at the edge of the square, so people are always within earshot. If, for some reason, things get out of hand, all you have to do is scream and they'll come running. I don't see you being in any danger, though."

"My thoughts exactly. We'll see what I might be able to get out of him."

"I'll walk you over there since I'm on my way out anyways." He dropped a quick kiss to my forehead. "I'm glad you're here, and despite what asshole Aden says, most of the pack truly does appreciate you."

Hand-in-hand, we walked across the square toward Aaron's temporary lodging. We waved to a few people and stopped to chat with others. Everyone had questions, which Isaiah answered truthfully, without giving away too much. His ability to do so impressed me.

Ten minutes later, we had talked to everyone who wanted to talk to him. He left me at the small porch of the guest house and waved goodbye. Once he was out of sight, I turned to knock on the door, surprised to see Aaron standing there with it wide open already.

"Ha! You startled me. That door didn't make a sound when it opened." I laughed. "I forget how stealthy you wolves can be when you want to be."

He echoed my laugh. "I wasn't even trying to be

stealthy. I just thought it would be polite to open the door, since I knew you were out here on the porch. Do you want to come in? If you're uncomfortable with that, we can stay on the porch, too."

"I'd love to come in, thanks. I happen to know that these guest homes are fully stocked, so maybe we could have a cup of tea or coffee?"

He stepped back and gestured for me to enter. "You're in luck. Not that I'm psychic or anything, but the first thing I did was start a pot of coffee, so it's ready to be poured. I also found some cookies in the pantry."

"Great. I love cookies."

Following him through the small living room, I tried to take in the details around me. The space was cozy, simply decorated, and made to ensure that any guest would feel welcome. I'd laughed at the notion that they had guest houses at all, considering how secretive they were, but apparently before the curse they did have guests from other packs as well as family members who had married and moved off the sanctuary come to visit. Isaiah had said they were sometimes also used for young ones who were ready to move out on their own before a new home could be built for them.

"Come in, have a seat. How do you take your coffee?" Aaron moved to the cupboard and grabbed me a mug.

"Very creamy and very sweet, please."

"Ah, a woman after my mother's own heart. I got my taste in java from my dad, straight black."

Once the coffees were ready, Aaron sat down across the table from me. Pulling my mother's magic close to me, I attempted to create a sound shield that would protect our conversation from the excellent hearing of anyone milling around. I don't know if Aaron felt the magic, but he didn't complain if he did. He met my eyes in a straightforward manner. Hoping he wouldn't be offended by my directness, I took a deep breath and jumped right in.

"I'd like to know a little bit more about your alpha and your pack, if that's okay."

"Sure. Anything in particular?"

"Well, I have no idea what there is to know, really. Which means I don't know which questions to ask. I've been told that the pack on the far side of the sanctuary is not just wolves. Is that true?"

Aaron smiled. "It is true. While we are mostly wolves, we have many other shifters within our group. A bear, a pair of condors, a couple different species of large cat, um... what else is there?" He paused for a minute and wrinkled his forehead. "Oh yeah, a raccoon and a wolverine family, too. I think that's about it, aside from the wolves, although I might have missed someone. We are fairly small compared to this pack, by the looks of it, anyway."

The idea perplexed me. My curiosity about other shifters engaged, and I wanted to know everything he would tell me, almost pushing aside my desire to know if their alpha might be my long-lost uncle. Trying not to seem overly nosy, I proceeded with my questions.

"And your alpha is a wolf? All the other animals are okay with that?"

"They agreed to it when they joined the pack. Many of the others do not live in groups that have an alpha, and they are fine with the setup because Rick is very respectful of their ways as well. He is more of a town mayor type than an actual alpha. The last alpha was more of a dictator, and not very well liked at all. Everyone is glad he's gone now."

"Was he very mean? Is that why the new alpha took over?"

Aaron inhaled deeply, then let it out slowly. He tapped his fingertips on the side of the coffee mug, quiet a minute before answering. "I was very young during his rule, so much of what I have heard is secondhand at best. But the story goes that he made some bad deals with outsiders that temporarily moved into the sanctuary. He became power hungry, and he sacrificed some of his pack to them in return for whatever they were offering. Nobody who was around then will confirm that, but I've heard enough variations of it to believe that the general premise is true."

The similarities between the story of the other pack and Isaiah's got my brain working overtime. Who were these mysterious outsiders? And what were they after that was so enticing for them to come in and try to destroy those who lived here to get it? Perhaps the two alphas had been working together. Maybe they had been competitors. It certainly needed more looking into.

"Rick hasn't always been part of our pack. I, at least, don't know where he was before coming to us, but I do vaguely remember when he first arrived. It was about the time outsiders started showing up more. He wandered into our territory weak and confused."

Stringing together what Aaron was telling me along with the facts my mother had given to me led me to believe that whatever had happened when Aimee's new husband left that day, it had been deliberate to get him away from her. After all, my grandmother had never approved of the marriage according to my mother, and she didn't sound like she'd ever been the most loving mother to Aimee and my mom anyways. I could see her being petty and taking any chance to destroy her happiness.

"At first," Aaron continued, "everyone was wary of him. The alpha had continuously warned the pack members to be afraid of all the new people infiltrating the sanctuary. He warned everyone that they had come to kidnap children and drain their powers. The longer Rick stayed, the more everyone began to trust him. After a few years, members of the pack began to look to him for his leadership and advice. The alpha didn't like that and threatened to expel him from the pack, but nobody would allow him to do that. They all swore they'd leave with him."

Aaron's story seemed to line up with what I had learned so far about the timeline of things deteriorating throughout the sanctuary as the evil spirit ramped up her attempts to regain her powers. The story itself was a little muddled, but as Aaron had said, he was young and only had stories told to him by others to go off. I would need to talk to someone who had more detailed memories of that time, to be sure.

"Nobody knows exactly what led up to the moment Rick actually challenged the old alpha, but he beat him. Usually those types of challenges are a fight to the death, but Rick showed him mercy and allowed him to live out the rest of his days in humiliation instead of killing him. He said there had been enough death among them, and he wasn't going to add to it."

"And has the new alpha been a better one, then? Those who live there are happy with him?"

"Oh yeah. There has been peace for years."

"If you were so happy with that pack and things have been so great, why would you even consider coming into another pack's territory just because you saw some weird weather over here? I'm sure there's been thunder and lightning in the area before. I've been around long enough to know that pack boundaries are pretty fiercely enforced."

He gave a sly smile. "I didn't lie to the elders when I explained how I got here. They would have known if I did."

"I wasn't accusing you of lying. I just really am curious."

"Honestly?"

"Of course, honestly. I wouldn't ask you a question just to hope you'd lie to me about it. That would be counter-productive."

"I wanted to meet you."

CHAPTER NINE

The hours of reading had not brought me to an answer for reversing the curse on the stream, but I now believed I knew how to remove enough of the curse from Isaiah to return his ability to shift. It would be a step in the right direction. Gathering the supplies listed in the grimoire and packing them into a backpack, I prepared to head into the woods and see if I could call Isaiah to me, the same way he was able to reach me.

Thankful that my aunt kept all of her spell casting supplies neat and orderly in her office so time wasn't wasted on searching for them, I added a couple sandwiches to the bag, as well as some bottled water. Pausing at the thought of how much effort the spell would take, whether or not it was successful, I added more food. A couple of apples, some cookies and a package of beef jerky gave me enough calories to at least make it home, I figured. With lunches packed, I was ready to get going.

Letting my mother know I'd be gone for a while, and ignoring her sour face at the news, I slipped out the backdoor. Perched on the table where I'd left the crackers sat my two little friends.

"Hey guys. Did you like the crackers?"

Both of them responded with chatter, one of them running in circles around the table top.

"Do you want some more?"

More chatter. More skittering about the table.

"Okay, be right back."

Taking a couple from each box I found to give them a variety, I returned to the porch. Laughing at myself for making conversation with the furry little creatures, I handed over the crackers and let them know I'd be gone for a while. At least they didn't seem to disapprove of my plans for the day.

Following the path into the woods, I reached out for Isaiah with my mind. I'd never tried to use our telepathy from a distance and didn't know what kind of range I had. It occurred to me then that I had also never been to the village where their houses were, which meant I couldn't just walk over and see if he happened to be home.

If he didn't hear me, or couldn't answer me, then I'd just be puttering around the yard until he showed up. Hopefully, he would have a reason to come by today. If not, I would just keep practicing until I saw him again.

After walking down the path for a few minutes, I could hear his voice, loud and clear.

"Hey. Are you okay, Leah?"

"Fine. But I have something exciting I want to try. Are you busy right now?"

"Not really, what's up? I can start heading your way."

"Good. I think today is the day. I believe I have a

spell so that I can return your ability to shift back to human form." My excitement bled into my tone, even telepathically.

"I'm on my way. Don't wander too far by yourself."

He came loping up the path minutes later. Somewhat unsuccessfully, I tried to hide how excited I was to see him. And how nervous I felt about the spell. It would be the most complicated one I had attempted to cast since learning about magic. Hopefully, I'd end up with a human at the end of it, and not a toad or a guinea pig.

Isaiah wanted to return to the clearing where we had sat before, and I agreed. Wherever he wanted me to perform the ritual was fine with me. Once we got there, I pulled out my aunt's book and the supplies. Each instruction was followed to the letter, and I kept up a running commentary, explaining what I had found out as I worked.

"I'm sorry, what?" Nothing in my power would have been able to hide the surprise in my voice or the shocked look that flooded my face. That answer was the last one I ever would have expected to come out of his mouth.

He moved his gaze to the table as if unwilling to meet my eyes once he'd made his admission. Keeping my attention on him, I leaned back in my chair and folded my arms over my chest. It took self-control to keep my mouth shut, but I managed it. Barely. The ball landed in his court and I expected him to volley it back.

He peeked sideways at me. "Are you angry?"

"I think I need more information from you before I can answer that honestly. I don't know what to think at the moment."

"Fair enough. I've been curious for a while now. When I was a child, there were stories about the crescent mark and those who were chosen to bear it. Rumor had it that the mark had returned and a new witch would bear the magic to combat the evil of the last mark holder. Then the stories died out because nobody in the sanctuary actually bore the mark of the goddess."

My hands remained tucked into my arms, my palm hidden. Unsure of whether the mark appeared in the same place for each chosen one, I didn't want him seeing my palm and knowing that mine was gone. Not yet.

"We all felt it when the guardian of the sanctuary died. It was like a rift tore open in the fabric of the magic that gives life to the sanctuary. Pain floated on the very air we breathed. She had not received the mark, and still she devoted her life to ensuring the sanctuary remained protected."

A tear slipped down my cheek. Aimee had touched so many lives. And while mystery still shrouded much of the situation of how she had lived here and not known that her love was just across the forest, it gave me some peace to know that the other pack knew of her and loved her for the sacrifices she made.

"Our alpha claims you are his kin. His niece from the marriage to his wife. We discussed how to make contact with you. He also claims you bear the mark. But I do not sense the sanctuary magic within you. Perhaps he was mistaken?"

Instinct kept me from revealing too much about myself to this complete stranger. Caution rushed over me. Trust hadn't been established firmly enough for me to reveal any personal information.

I sidestepped the obvious question. "If I am correct, your alpha was once married to my aunt Aimee, the former guardian of the sanctuary. But he disappeared years ago. I assume around the time he showed up to your pack, and she never saw him again."

Anger flooded me for the pain he caused her. What kind of man runs out on his wife and never returns? Especially hiding in plain sight, within walking distance of her? He had to have known that she spent months, if not years, searching for him. And yet he evaded her at every turn. What an asshole. Aaron nodded at my statement, making me wonder if he knew more about that situation than he was letting on.

"Rick knew that once you were here, the Western pack would convince you to help them. We all knew about the curse that plagued their pack. Very few of our pack were affected because we drink from the water at the falls, the source. Our small territory is protected by the very magic that created the sanctuary."

His explanation surprised me. Before now, I'd only been able to guess whether any of the others that lived in the sanctuary had been affected by the curse. It hadn't been clear whether the curse had targeted this pack specifically, or how the actual curse had been directed. Pieces of the puzzle kept appearing, but I didn't have enough to make a clear picture yet.

"He feared that by getting involved with the breaking of the curse that the sanctuary would find you in disfavor and you would lose your mark. The mark itself is granted to those with the best interest of the land in their hearts. Because this pack had once aligned with the evil spirit, he feared that helping them would cost you."

Surprise turned to shock. Aaron's explanations were giving me more questions than answers. How had my uncle known all this? And if he had been aware, why hadn't he tried to make contact with me sooner to prevent me from losing the mark? For every piece of the puzzle I gathered, it seemed like the size of the puzzle itself expanded and required me to find ten more. The thought of ever getting all the information I needed exhausted me.

"I want nothing more than to protect the sanctuary. I thought I was doing that by breaking the curse. Why didn't he come to me before all of that happened and tell me this himself?"

"I can't answer all the questions for you. Most of those answers will have to come from the alpha himself. I'm just sharing with you the little information that was passed on to me, and that bit is far from everything there is to know."

We finished our coffee in relative silence; me pondering the new information he had given me, and him quietly eating cookies. The silence wasn't uncomfortable, and I made no effort to fill it. We'd been sitting at that table for over two hours when I felt Isaiah return to the village. He checked to see if I was still here, and confirmed he'd be over in a minute when I confirmed my location to him.

Aaron answered the sharp knock at the door with a shout to come in, and Isaiah came strolling into the kitchen. Nobody else followed him. Our eyes met, and I tried to read his expression. His gaze shifted to Aaron.

"We searched the area around the temple yard. There are no outward signs of a scuffle there, but we did find drag marks from the direction of the stream to the wall near where we found you."

"I told you I wasn't lying to you."

"I never said you were lying. But you don't remember, either, so we were hoping to get a few more clues as to what really happened, for our information and yours. I'm sorry to say there wasn't a whole lot to learn there."

"I really wish I could help you more. I'm not a huge fan of not knowing what the heck happened to me, either."

"I totally understand. We'll do what we can to get some answers for you, if they're there to find. For now, you are welcome to stay here and continue to heal and rest."

"I appreciate your hospitality."

Aaron's gaze darted between Isaiah and I, as if he expected me to immediately spill the information that he had given me. The longer I stayed quiet, the more confused he became. At no point did he draw attention to our conversation, though, unwilling to draw attention to the possibility that he told me things that he didn't necessarily want Isaiah to know.

Isaiah asked if I was ready to leave, and we said our goodbyes. I let Aaron know that I'd be back to visit with him while he was here. He waved and let us see ourselves out as he continued to eat the cookies straight from the package.

As we crossed the square back to Isaiah's office, I mulled over the conversation I had with Aaron and how much of it I wanted to share with Isaiah. Seeds of doubt had been sown, and I struggled with the desire to keep all the information to myself. He already knew about the alpha being my uncle, though, which meant I could give him many details without him suspecting that I was holding out on him. I just needed to be sure that I kept up a wall in my thoughts so he didn't catch me off guard, and the extra information didn't leak out.

"Is their alpha actually your missing uncle?" Apparently, he could read my mind, latching onto the only pieces of information that I decided to give him.

"Yes. He seems to be, strangely enough. It's so weird to think that he has been just across the peninsula all this time. She looked everywhere for him and he was right there."

"Did the kid say why he stayed there and didn't go back to her?"

"No. he told me he couldn't answer that. I'd have to ask my uncle for any of the reasons for his private decisions."

"That makes sense. I can't see a man of your uncle's age confiding about his personal life to a kid."

"Right? And Aaron said he was so young when Rick became the alpha. Before that happened, he didn't know much of anything about him. He did say that the previous alpha was making deals with outsiders, similar to yours. I wonder if they were working together, or on their own?"

Isaiah's face tightened at the question. The change was almost imperceptible, and if I hadn't been studying him so closely at right that minute, I would have missed it entirely. When he answered me, all traces of the change were gone and he continued on casually.

"I'd guess separately, but I can't say for sure either way. There is a lot we don't know about what went on with the outsiders. The sheer volume of rumors at the time made it close to impossible to distinguish fact from fiction."

"Right? It's so hard to know what to believe." The irony of that statement was not lost on me as the words passed through my lips.

"Hopefully, someday, we'll get enough answers to at least have a good idea about some of the stuff that went on."

We stopped at the porch of the office building. He had work to do and, despite the tension between my mother and me, I needed to get home. The hidden room in the basement was calling to me, and I wanted to scour the family books to see if I could figure out more information about the other pack from them.

"Did he say anything else while you were there?" Finally, he asked the question I'd been expecting since we left the guest house.

"Not really. He answered my questions when he could, but he didn't have much information that we would be interested in. Unfortunately, he is pretty much just a kid, which means he isn't privy to much of the juicy information that we'd want to hear about."

Keeping my voice level took effort, and I hoped it didn't make Isaiah suspicious. He invited me in, but I declined, citing the need to get home and look for more clues. He didn't argue.

"Want me to walk you back?"

"Oh, you know I'd love that, but I don't want to take you away from the work you need to be doing here. Let's not give any more members of the pack reason to say you're shirking your duties because of me."

He rolled his eyes, but agreed, his tone dry. "You'll let me know when you get home, right? Then I don't have to worry."

"I will, for sure. And later I plan to spend some time in the hidden room in the basement, so if you can't reach me, that's why. No need to worry."

"Good to know. I might have worried again." He winked.

His response made a little tug of guilt in my stomach, but I ignored it. With a small smile, I turned to head across the square and back toward the trail that led home. He grabbed my hand and pulled me close for a hug. I let him, but my response was half-hearted at best.

"Everything okay?"

"Of course, just thinking about getting home and dealing with my mom again. I wish she'd come around to see my way of things for real. But she may be able to confirm or disprove some of the theories I have after talking to Aaron, so I need to do it. See you soon?"

He agreed, and I could feel him watching me as I walked away. I waved to Shelby, who was perched on a bench, and promised I'd be back soon. The walk home left me time to ponder the news Aaron had sprung me.

My uncle not only knew I was here, but that Aimee had died and I had lost my mark. I wondered if he also knew who the evil spirit really was. And if he did, had that factored into his decision to stay with the pack instead of returning to his new wife and their life together? Did he have more of a connection to the evil spirit than anyone knew?

CHAPTER TEN

The glade was shrouded in an eerie silence as I left the trail and crossed over to the house. My resident chipmunk pair was holed up elsewhere and all the windows facing this side of the forest were dark. I could sense my mother in the house, and felt her magic being drawn toward her, as if it wanted to make its way home.

Before I made it to the back porch, the air in the vicinity became oppressive. The sudden sensation took my breath away and had I not known better, I would have sworn a bus just parked itself on my chest. Forcing my legs, which weighed a hundred pounds a piece, to move my body toward the safety of the house seemed impossible. Panic set in. The security we set up should have prevented anything like this from being able to reach me.

Air currents swirled around me, tugging at my hair and pelting me with dry pine needles. Each one felt like tiny zaps of lightning against my skin. Soft laughter echoed in my ears.

"Let me go," I ground out between my clenched teeth.

More laughter was my only response. Air buffeted me back and forth, icy fingers plucking at my clothes and poking at my exposed skin. The ring on my finger warmed as I drew on my borrowed magic. The sensation built inside me until suddenly sparking outward, shoving the evil spirit back.

The force of it propelled me forward, arms and legs akimbo, as I ate dirt about five feet from the back steps. Damn my klutzy nature. The bridge of my nose stung as I spat out pebbles and attempted to sit up.

More soft laughter crooned in my ear. "I am

gaining power, child. Pretty soon there will be nowhere on Earth you will be safe. Your pretty mother is already in danger," the voice trailed off as the winds died completely and the night air returned to normal.

Not even bothering to get completely to my feet, I scrambled up the stairs and let myself in, slamming the back door behind me. The sudden bang drew my mother's attention from the living room. Before I could call out to her, she appeared in the doorway.

"What in heaven's name is going on?" She flipped the light switch and gasped at the sight of me.

"You didn't sense anything strange just now?" I began to question her as she grabbed a clean rag and wet it at the sink, crossing over to press it to my nose. "Ow! That stings!"

She shook her head. "Nothing was amiss until you came barreling through the door like a forest fire raged behind you. Why?"

"The evil spirit. She was able to get to me in the clearing. She said her power is growing and soon there will be nowhere I would be safe." I left out the part about her threatening my mom. She didn't need anything else to worry about at the moment.

Her brow creased, and she silently dabbed at my wound for a few seconds before replying. "I knew we wouldn't have much time. She is capable of sucking power from wherever she finds it if it's not well protected. We need to stop her while she is still confined to the sanctuary. If she gets out, it will be over. There will be no stopping her."

"Okay, but how?"

While I waited for her answer, I argued with myself about how much I should tell her from the conversation I'd had with Aaron earlier. Would she tell me to stay away from the other pack? Or would she encourage me to find answers, if possible? The last thing I wanted was for her to insist on coming with me if I went to look for Rick.

"I don't know yet." Her shoulder slumped, and she gripped the damp rag tight enough to squeeze a stream of water out onto the floor. "I just don't know."

"Let's get some sleep. We can figure it out tomorrow. I'm too sore to think much now anyways."

At her nod, I stepped toward the hallway,

forgetting about the puddle of water at my feet. My foot slid across the floor. Arms pinwheeling, I attempted to catch myself on the dining chair, only to find it toppling down with me. Attempting to catch me brought my mother right down on top of me with an "Oomph."

Choking on a groan, I pushed at her. "Off. Me."

Sliding to the side, she reached out and moved the chair out of our space. "Sorry, honey. I thought I could help."

Both of us remained down, quiet except for some slightly heavy breathing. The water previously on the floor soaked into the back of my pants, spreading as I sat in it. A sigh escaped. If I ever got my magic back, I was going to find a way to be less clumsy.

By the time the two if us managed to get to our feet, I'd had enough of the day. Sleep might not fix all my problems, but nothing else was going to get accomplished until I'd gotten some. Bidding my mother goodnight, I trudged to my bed, shimmying out of the wet pants and leaving them in a heap on the floor. They were a tomorrow problem.

Icy pinpricks scuttled across my bare legs. The

sensation caused me to jerk fully awake, confusion plaguing me when I couldn't reach down to brush it away. My limbs lay useless, refusing to obey my commands to move. Nary a twitch in response to my efforts. Only my eyes could move.

Not that my view relieved the building panic. Icy blue-white mist swirled around me, blocking the sight of anything else. An elephant could have been standing an inch from my nose and I wouldn't even know it. I couldn't even be sure where I was. My bedroom? Had the spirit been able to invade the house itself? Or the dreamscape? I'd been here numerous times before, but each situation had been different.

When my voice didn't work, I reached out with my senses. Something else shared the space, whether I could see it or not. The surface I lay on trembled ever so slightly beneath my cheek. Dread crawled up my throat, choking me. My lungs refused to expand and lack of oxygen began to make me woozy.

My connection to Isaiah remained dark. My tongue felt so thick in my mouth it couldn't have formed words even if it did move. My eyelids continued to droop despite my struggle to keep them open. Despair settled in. I was losing a battle I hadn't even had a chance to fight.

Violent shaking rattled my brain. "Leah!"

I took a huge gulp of air, and then another, before opening my eyes. My mother's worried face loomed above me, out of focus but familiar. She had tears running down her cheeks.

"Thank the goddess." She flung herself across me and sobbed.

Too disoriented to question her immediately, I lay beneath her and attempted to get my bearings. I could see that we were in my room, and I knew we lay on my bed. But what the hell had just happened?

As her quaking eased, I pushed against her feebly. Breathing came difficult enough without her constricting my movements. She sat up, shoving her hair out of her face. Reaching out, she grabbed by cheeks with both hands, studying me. Her eyes searched mine, then ran over my face and body. Her head shook side to side slowly, almost as if she didn't realize she was doing it.

"What?" My voice came out scratchy and

painful. My throat felt like I had swallowed a cheese grater, gotten it stuck and spent an hour trying to drag it out. My lips cracked with the small movement of forming the single word, and I could feel the small droplet of blood gather at the corner of my mouth. It was becoming apparent that I was in pretty bad shape.

"I thought I'd lost you."

She pulled back her hands, not removing her gaze. My hands shook as I attempted to reach out to her. But at least they moved. Or tried to. To say I was weak would be an understatement of the most obvious kind. I gave up and lay quietly, waiting for her to compose herself enough to tell me what had happened while I thought I'd been sleeping.

Pursing her lips, she blew out a breath, inhaling deeply before beginning. "I heard you screaming. Over and over you screamed. By the time I got in here, you had stopped. You were so cold." She shuddered. "Nothing I did would wake you. Then you quit breathing."

Remembering my inability to make any sounds in the dreamscape, I silently thanked the goddess that my physical body had been making decisions of its own accord. If not for the screams, my mother never would have come to check on me and I very well may have died. But how did she get me breathing again?

As if sensing my confusion, she continued. "I had to shock you with my magic to get you to take a breath. Then I had to do it again before you began to do it on your own."

No wonder I felt as if I had been electrocuted, on top of all the other ailments making themselves known. These last couple of days had not been easy on my physical body. Would my mind be next?

"Water?" I needed something to quench the sandpaper-y feel of my raw throat. At least I knew it had been the screaming to cause it, and I didn't have to wonder what happened.

"Of course!" Mom jumped up and grabbed the glass off my bedside table, disappearing through the door and returning within a minute. "Let me help you sit up."

Between the two of us, we managed to get me mostly upright, although not enough to prevent a good bit of the water from dribbling down my chin and soaking into the front of my shirt. Feeling like an invalid sucked.

An hour later, I had enough strength for her to help me to the bathroom to shower, where I hoped to wash away at least some aches and pains, not to mention removing the dirt and debris from my hair. Gripping the edge of the sink for support, I stared at myself in the mirror while I waited for the water to heat. The scrape across the bridge of my nose screamed raw and red against my pale skin. Said pale skin also accentuated the deep discoloration beneath my eyes, with a lack of sleep contributing to the bruising from yesterday's fall in the yard. With the pine needles and twigs sticking out from my messy hair, the grand and terrifying baba yaga had nothing on me.

Thankful I didn't need to maneuver my way over the edge of a tub, I hobbled into the shower. The warm water ran down as I washed. It turned from a cloudy gray-brown to clear again. Unable to lift my arms well enough to wash my hair, I simply stood under the spray until I felt like the majority of the hangers-on had been evicted. Good enough.

A handful of conditioner got somewhat rubbed in before I hurt too bad to do anything more, and I sunk to the bottom of the shower, covered my face with my hands, and let myself cry it out. Crying for Aimee, who I would never see again. Crying at the pain. Crying at my own insecurities. It seemed more and more likely that I would never have enough power to stop the evil spirit before she took over the entire sanctuary.

The water ran cold before I ran out of tears, bringing an end to my shower pity party. I managed to dry off, wrangle my wet hair into a messy bun and get some clothes on just as my mom came knocking to see if I was okay.

"I'm still alive, don't worry," I called through the door. At least the steam from the shower had helped my throat and my parched lips. Unfortunately, it hadn't done much for my overall appearance. Not that I cared. Who did I have to impress anyways?

"Okay. Let me know if you need any help. I'm just finishing up brunch if you're hungry."

We ate in silence, my mother looking me over as I struggled to behave normally. Once I had a little food in me, I felt almost human once more. Like a miserable human who'd had their ass beat, but human none-the-less. Better than the pile of shit I had felt like earlier.

My mom looked at me sadly. "The coroner will deliver Aimee's body to us today. Her last wishes were to be buried here on the sanctuary, beneath the trees at the far side of the house."

"Should we have some type of funeral for her? I know the packs will want to pay their final respects."

She hesitated before shaking her head. "I don't think now is a good time. Perhaps we can bury her, and then, later when it's safe, we can have a memorial for her."

As much as I wanted to argue with her, she made sense. Aimee would probably agree with her too, despite their disagreements.

As I ate, the need to go and talk to Aaron again became more insistent. He had more information that I needed, whether he realized it or not, and my desire to figure it out grew exponentially the more I thought about it.

My mother tried to convince me not to leave the

house. "You need to rest and recover. You can't go gallivanting all over the forest in your condition."

"Seriously. This again? We both know we have no time to waste. If I don't get moving and figure this out, simple rest and recovery won't be able to save me next time. I'll be back."

Before I could march out the back door, there was a knock at the front. Remembering my last instance opening the door, I hung back and allowed my mother to answer it. An ambulance sat parked in the drive, and my heart clenched at the sight of it. Aimee was in there.

Silently, I hung back and let my mother handle it. She directed them to the spot she had mentioned earlier as I followed. To my surprise, a deep hole already yawned open in the dirt. The crew from the ambulance lowered the black vinyl bag to the bottom, offering more assistance if we needed it.

My mother politely declined, sending them on their way. Looking into the hole, the idea of leaving her in a bag made me shudder.

"We aren't..."

"No. Absolutely not." Waving her hand and

murmuring a spell, my mother made use of her magic right in front of me, in one of the very first times I was able to pay attention.

The click black vinyl morphed into satin and lace. She turned to me and gave a small smile.

"The spell was Aimee's. She had everything set up in advance, so all we had to do was say the words." Her grief came through heavily in her voice.

"Can I see her?" My voice trembled as I asked.

"Do you really want to?"

I hesitated, then nodded. "Yes. The last picture of her I have in my head is her laying on the floor in the temple. At least this way I can see her at peace."

With a soft command from my mother, the satin floated back, revealing Aimee's beautiful face. She looked exactly as I had seen her during our last visit. To avoid crying, I bit my cheek hard enough to draw blood. All of a sudden, the reality that she would never leave this spot smacked me in the face.

She really was gone. Even seeing her body in the temple, I hadn't accepted the reality of it. Here and now, as we prepared to bury her in the earth of the land she had loved so much, it became jarringly, painfully real.

"Are you ready?" My mother was gentle in her inquiry.

No. I wasn't. But that didn't matter. It was time. "We have to do it, whether I am ready or not. We can't stop at this point."

The final words of whatever spell Aimee had woven in advance floated on the air as my mom whispered them. The satin wrapped lovingly around her, protecting her skin from the dirt that filled the hole one final time. Wrapping our arms around each other, we stood at the edge of the site and cried together.

"Goodbye, Aimee. I love you."

My mom sniffled as I wiped my cheeks. "I'm sorry, Mom. I need to get out of here. Just for a little bit. I'm going for a walk to clear my head."

She didn't argue this time as I turned on my heel and headed toward the woods. As guilty as I felt for abandoning her right after we buried her only sister, I couldn't bear to be in the vicinity of the grave at that moment. I needed distance to help dull the pain.

My purposeful strides lasted until I rounded the

corner in the path and the trees blocked me from her view. Once I knew she couldn't see me, I sagged, resting my hands on my knees and trying to gather the energy I would need to make it to the village.

In a moment of insanity, I considered trying to shift into a wolf so I could run the entire way, but the fear of getting stuck in that form had me dismissing the thought almost immediately. That and the realization that I didn't want to end up naked in the pack house when (and if) I turned human again. My feet were just going to have to suck it up and make it.

I didn't announce myself to Isaiah when I arrived, although I knew he must have felt me. Making a beeline for the guest cabin Aaron occupied, I gave little more than brief greetings as I passed people I knew. The need for information surpassed my desire to be polite.

The door opened before I had a chance to knock. Aaron's face peered through the opening. "Come in. What the heck happened to you?"

Pushing the door closed behind me, I followed him to the table and sank into the chair across from him before I answered. He watched me intently, waiting quietly.

"It's a long story. Let's just say I had a rough night last night."

His lips quirked up into an almost smirk before smoothing out. If I hadn't been staring right at him, I would have missed it. His eyes rippled blue, before a blink returned them to normal. Refusing to make anything of it, I looked at him with eyebrows raised at his response.

"Did you now?"

CHAPTER ELEVEN

Something in the back of my mind prompted me to reserve the words that I'd been about to let loose about my dreams the previous night. Unable to pinpoint the cause of my sudden case of nerves, I just smiled a wry smile at him and nodded. Who was I to argue with such a strong sense of intuition at this point in my journey?

Aaron handed me a cup of coffee, piping hot, and made to my liking. Sipping the steaming liquid, I waited for my thoughts to settle themselves before trying to determine how to steer the conversation in the direction I wished it to go. He seemed to be in no hurry to break the silence and waited without prompting.

"How did you sleep, being in a strange house in a strange place?" Small talked seemed a safe enough opening to me.

"Fine. I felt a little on edge, but must have needed the sleep because once I dozed off I slept like the dead. Even the goddess herself couldn't have woken me."

Conversation meandered aimlessly from subject to subject as I tried to feel him out and get an idea of whether I could really trust him. Not that I felt as if I had much choice. He was the key to getting to the other pack and meeting my uncle. The answers I needed lay through him either way.

I filled him in on some of the details of how I broke the curse and what had happened after, skirting the issue of losing my mark. We took turns asking questions of each other as the morning wore on.

"You know," he interrupted my thoughts, "I am

not here to cause harm. I don't want to create trouble for this pack or you. I wasn't sent here to spy on you guys or anything of that nature."

"I believe you," I slowly answered him, wondering why he felt the need to bring it up again.

"Can I ask you a question?" His gazed pierced mine, eyes seeming bluer than they had been a moment before.

I hesitated. "Sure. I guess so."

"Does it bother you? The way a lot of the pack members still treat you? Even after all you did for them."

The snort escaped me before I could contain it. "Honestly? Yeah, it does. Especially that some of them are spreading rumors and telling lies, after what I sacrificed to break the curse. I try not to take it personally, but sometimes I can't help it. Then I feel bad for Isaiah trying to find a balance between helping me and being loyal to his pack."

"Do you trust them?"

Unease slid through me at the question, feelings of uncertainty I'd been trying to bury bubbling to the surface. "Isaiah, absolutely. Without a doubt."

"And the others?" Aaron waited for my answer, his gaze weighing heavy on my own.

Torn between being honest and feeling the need for secrecy, I waffled. "I barely know any of the others..." I hesitated before continuing. "It wouldn't be fair to make a judgment on the very little I have to go on."

Aaron didn't respond, just watched me with his icy eyes. Something in them made me feel like he hoped to be able to read my deepest secrets if he looked hard enough. My lips curled into a grimace and I shrugged.

"I'd be lying if I said I didn't feel wary of them, though."

His nod was the only indicator he heard me for a whole minute. Shaking himself, he changed the subject, and we chatted until I felt like I needed to leave. Isaiah indicated he was in a meeting he couldn't get out of, and I promised to see him the next time I came over.

The next few days flew by as I spent time visiting Aaron, arguing with my mother and feeling out the capabilities of my borrowed magic. It fought me as often as it cooperated, and I couldn't tell if it stemmed from a lack of mastery on my own part or the finicky nature of the gift itself. Either way, frustration hovered over me constantly.

Aaron had been a guest in the shifter village for almost a week before our conversation turned in the direction I'd been dreading. Doubt about the pack plagued me, both in my dreams and during my waking hours. The next tidbit of information tore open the metaphorically festering wound.

"Can I tell you a secret?"

My eyes met his. I searched them for a long minute before nodding.

"I think there are traitors among the pack." He held up his hand to stop me from protesting, and I pressed my lips together, waiting for him to finish. "There are men of this pack who don't believe Isaiah to be a capable alpha. I think they are sowing dissent among the others. At least some of them are keeping secrets."

"And how do you know this?" In a way, it felt gratifying that someone other than myself thought similarly, but I wanted nothing more than to be wrong.

"Obviously, I am a stranger, so no one is in here confessing their deepest, darkest secrets to me. But I sleep very little, and I am observant. Tiny little whispers spread like wildfire, but never enough to pinpoint any single person to be starting them."

My mother's magic trembled, feeling like buzzing vibrations in my core. Unfortunately, I didn't know it well enough to understand if it was in agreement or not with his statement. Pinning my bottom lip between my teeth, I debated on how to respond. For as much as I didn't know many of the members of Isaiah's pack, I didn't know Aaron either.

My hesitation must have been obvious, because he pushed on without waiting for me to respond.

"Many of the current members of the pack were around when a select group began allowing outsiders to infiltrate the reserve. I have no doubt many of them are still here to this day. I think something like that may be happening again. I don't think the members of the reserve are the only ones here now."

"But, before, wasn't it only the influence of the evil spirit that caused them to do those things? Do you think she is able to get to them again?"

"The spirit can only corrupt if the seed is there to begin with. She can take that seed and nurture it, force it to grow and spread, but she can't plant it. Whoever has been letting them enter the reserve has to have a reason of their own for doing so."

My inhale whistled through pursed lips. "How? How do you know? And are you sure they're here?"

"I don't know for sure. But I keep getting hints of smells that don't belong, especially after certain members come back from being gone for a while. I haven't shifted since I have been here, as it is considered rude to do so when not invited when you are not on your home territory, so I am without many of the senses I might use to investigate. I might be young, but I am not ignorant."

"I didn't mean to imply you were. I simply don't understand how you are catching something Isaiah is not."

"Who's to say he isn't? He and I are not sitting and having tea together every afternoon like old friends. He may be aware. He may not. I just wanted to share with you what I suspect."

Silence stretched between us. Indecision soured my stomach. Should I tell Isaiah what Aaron had shared with me? Would he even believe me? It's not like the information came from a trusted source. Blood pounded in my ears and I rubbed my temples. I needed to get home and rest so I could think clearly.

I stood, pushing back my chair. "I think I'd better go. I need some time to think. But I'll be back soon."

He didn't argue or get up from his chair. Closing the door behind me, I stepped off the small porch, running nose first into Isaiah. The collision caught me off guard. My face crashed into his solid chest and the impact knocked me backwards. Grace, being my ever-constant companion, I managed to catch my heel and the last stair, losing my balance.

Somehow, the shoe that got caught on the stairs flew to the left, the rest of me pitching to the right. I let out a yelp of surprise. My hands slammed into the dirt, and an audible cracking sound accompanied the searing pain. My right wrist buckled beneath my weight, leaving it up to my face to "catch" me in the dirt.

Aaron appeared in the doorway as Isaiah reached

out to help me up with my good arm. For a brief moment, the scrapes imitated the itchy throbbing of the mark on my palm, momentarily distracting me from the pain. Coincidence was all it was, and the stabbing agony returned full force.

"Are you alright?" Aaron inquired from the doorway. Isaiah's dirty look stopping him from coming any closer.

"She's fine. I'll take care of her."

Isaiah practically dragged me off as I cast an apologetic look over my shoulder. A couple of other pack members looked our way, but didn't approach. Heading into the alpha office, he shoved the door shut behind us with a bang and turned to look at me as he perched on the edge of the desk. I sank into the chair; the pain getting to me.

Cradling my aching arm against me, I glared at him. "Oh, I'm just fine. Thank you very much for asking. I can see how you would be concerned, seeing as how **you** are the one who knocked me down."

"Aren't you used to falling by now? You do it all the time."

His tone struck me and I gasped as if he'd slapped

my face. The words were no joke, and I stared back at him, surprise stealing the words from me momentarily. What the hell had gotten into him?

"Excuse me? What the hell is your problem?" Anger overrode the pain.

"You think I don't realize all the time you spend with your new friend? You sneak over here and shut yourself in the house with him, putting up your little bubble so that nobody can hear what you are in there talking about. Did you really think that you two being in cahoots would go unnoticed?"

"Excuse me?" I repeated myself, astonishment bringing on a lack of vocabulary to adequately express just how pissed off he was making me.

His eyes bore into mine. I could almost see the emotion crashing like in them like waves against the shore. He didn't add to his accusation, just stared at me, as if he waited for me to confess some damning secret.

Ignoring the pain, I pushed to my feet and headed toward the door. Nobody, even an *alpha,* talked to me like that and got away with it. I'd share what Aaron had told me after he apologized.

Before I could blink, he stood in front of me, blocking the way.

"Move."

He didn't budge. Nor did he speak. My temper soared. Using my good arm, I reached out and gave him a shove. As soon as I connected with him, magic arced between us, sending him flying sideways into the wall. In spite of my shock at its help, I turned to tell him off.

"Don't you try to bully me, *Alpha*," I sneered. I stalked out of the room, throwing my words behind me. "When you feel like apologizing, I'd be happy to fill you in. Until then, you can stay the hell away from me."

"Fine." His words thundered through the room, echoing off the walls. "You are no longer welcome here. Don't come back."

A different kind of pain sliced through me at his words, but I didn't let them slow me down. More of the pack had made their way to the central grassland, some of them looking on in shock, others smirking as I passed by. Refusing to dignify their attention, I stalked across the invisible border, hurrying to blend in with the trees and disappear from sight.

Once I knew I was far out of their radius of senses, I paused. Leaning up against a tree, I let the tears flow. The anger could only carry me so far before the double-edged pain of physical and emotional wounds became too much. My nose already felt swollen and tender. My head pounded and my wrist ached. Every cell in my body suddenly drooped with exhaustion. And I still had a long walk back.

CHAPTER TWELVE

Using my sleeve, I wiped the tears and at least some of the dirt from my cheeks. Time to head back to the house and face the music. With this magic, I couldn't heal myself, and I needed to swallow my pride and ask my mother for her help, in spite of us not being on the best of terms lately. The wrist wasn't broken; I didn't think, but it hurt like the dickens and I had no desire to wait for time to do its job. Something told me there wasn't much time to be had at all before the next trying thing presented itself.

By the time I reached the path leading to the house, I'd begun stumbling with exhaustion. Each step sent pain ricocheting up my arm and into my head. Added to the tears of betrayal from Isaiah's treatment and I had a pounding headache. For a few minutes I stood in the treeline, staring. A few lights were on, but I couldn't see my mother through any of the windows.

Daylight hadn't quite begun to wane yet, but the shadows still seemed to lengthen as I watched. Avoiding looking toward the area where we had laid Aimee to rest, I focused on the house itself. Nothing sinister jumped out at me.

Swallowing yet another exasperated sigh, I trudged across the clearing to the porch. Suspicious splotches of a thick, dark liquid lay on the step and decking. Leaning down to get a closer look, I straightened suddenly, and painfully, when it became obvious it was blood.

"Mom?" I rushed to the back door, reaching out with my injured arm and crying out in pain. Using the good hand, I flung the door open and called out for her again. "Mom!"

Hurried footsteps came from the hall. "Leah? What in heaven's name is wrong?" She pulled up short and stared at me. "What happened to you?"

Tears fell again at seeing she was alright. "There is blood all over the porch. I thought something awful had happened to you!"

She shook her head. "I'm fine," she soothed me with her tone as she had when I was a little girl. "Come, sit." She tried to grab my wrist, stopping as she saw me wince in pain. "Again, what happened to you? Not all of this-" she waved her hand in my direction, "came from finding some blood on our porch."

"Today was shit. Isaiah is a ginormous shit. And being clumsy is a pain in the damn ass." I sniffled.

"Tell me all about it so I can help you fix it." My mother used her crooning voice, one I hadn't heard since my age was a single digit number, and I used to have nightmares that caused me to wake up screaming in the middle of the night.

"First, why is there blood on the porch? Do you have any idea where it came from?"

"No." She raised her eyebrows. "Now, are you

going to tell me what happened?"

I gave her the abbreviated version, leaving out much of the detail but managing to cover most of my trials with broad sweeping strokes of explanation that were enough to satisfy her. She took my wrist gently, feeling for broken bones. The corners of her lips turned downward as I winced.

"I can heal you most of the way up, but it's going to hurt something fierce, and you'll probably want to rest so you can get well quicker."

"I haven't got any pressing errands to do anyways."

As much as I worried about the fact that the only other person in this house would be my mother, who I hadn't gotten along with well as of late, the idea of taking a day or two to figure some things out sounded like a good idea. If I couldn't go back to the pack village, I would need to find a way to communicate with Aaron. Sharp pain in my arm brought my focus back to the situation at hand.

"I told you it was going to hurt. Now sit still and give me your arm back. I can't heal it if I'm not touching it."

Gritting my teeth, I allowed her to pull it closer to her and waited. The initial jolt of discomfort had nothing on the fire that crawled through my bone as she chanted. While localized, the pain sent radiating waves up my arm into my shoulder and then across my chest and back. Sweat beaded on my forehead. My eyes shut so tightly I felt like the eyelids were turning inside out.

About the time I decided I'd rather leave it injured and wait for time to do its thing, the fire went out. It left behind an ache hovering at the level of a dull roar, but I considered it an improvement of only a slight one for the moment.

"Now, let me look at your nose. It looks like you are going to have two black eyes to go with it."

My hands shot up to protect my face. "No! Thank you. But no. That's not nearly so bad. I can just wait for it to heal by itself." The thought of those flames of pain crawling across my face just about did me in. Absolutely not.

She pressed her lips together. "Hmph."

"Honestly, mom, thank you. But my face is fine."

She stood, looking down at me. "It's your call, but

I'd at least put some ice on it."

"Good idea. Ice and ibuprofen. Then a nap."

Maybe I would sleep all the way until tomorrow. Or the next day. Maybe next week? All I wanted at that moment was to forget the pain, forget how angry I was at Isaiah, and forget that I still had to deal with the evil spirit of my godforsaken grandmother before she managed to ruin everything and probably kill us all.

The trudge to my bed seemed longer than any hallway in the history of the world. Skipping trying to change my clothes, all I did was lay back and position the ice pack on my aching face, hoping that the swelling would abate by the time I needed to be seen by anyone else.

While dreamless, my sleep turned out to be a relentless storm of tossing and turning, never quite leading to any true rest. For the rest of the day and an entire night, I attempted to sleep and never quite succeeded. I dozed off a few times, enough to feel like I jerked awake, but never really slept. The sensation drove me crazy.

Upon "waking" for the morning (read, giving up

on sleep) it became apparent that while my mom had healed the bone in my arm, the rest of my aches and pains were unaffected. Everything hurt. A glance in the bathroom mirror told me I looked about as crappy as I felt. As predicted, double bruises taunted me from under my already puffy eyes and swollen nose.

Huffing indignantly and mumbling under my breath, I wrenched the shower on as hot as I could stand it and stepped in. A sigh slipped out as I tried to relax. Leaning against the shower wall, I closed my eyes and took deep breaths. Within seconds, the water in the shower turned ice cold.

Shivering and yelping at the onslaught of the icy droplets, I attempted to turn the temperature up, thinking perhaps my mother had turned on the dishwasher or washing machine. When I reached the maximum temperature without any improvement, I shut it off. In my rush to get out of the cold, I slammed my big toe into the side of the shower and ripped my nail, blood flowing onto the floor and rug.

Cussing, I reached for some toilet paper before noticing a strange blue haze in the condensation on the mirror. Soft laughter echoed in my ears. Checking to be sure nobody had snuck in behind me, I called out.

"Who's here?"

The quiet laughter continued, mocking and unnerving me. Staring into the mirror, I attempted to see if I could make out any forms, but nothing presented itself. The blue haze winked out of existence and the laughter trailed off into silence. Grimacing, I tended to my throbbing toe and wrapped myself in a towel.

Not once did I question who invaded my space, but I sure wanted to know how the hell she got by the wards and protections that we worked so hard on keeping her out. We needed to reinforce them before something even worse happened. The house couldn't be our safe space if she could get in.

My mom sat at the table, nursing a cup of coffee and staring into space as I walked in. For a minute, it didn't even seem like she realized I was talking to her. After my first couple sentences she shook herself, somewhat sharply, splashing coffee over the rim of her mug and onto the tabletop. She stared at it, confused, as the puddle widened in front of her.

"Mom! Are you okay?" I grabbed a couple of napkins and pressed them onto the spill.

"I think so? That was weird. I could hear you, and see you, but you didn't seem to really be here."

"The wards are failing and we have to do something about it."

"You did end up with black eyes, just like I suspected." She murmured the words, as if she hadn't heard mine just seconds before.

"Mother! Are you listening to me?"

Her eyes jerked to mine. "Yes. Why, pray tell, are you shouting at me?"

"What did I just say?" I waited, searching her face for any sign that something more was off than just her inability to pay attention.

"Um, I don't know. Tell me again. I'm sorry. Sleep was impossible last night, no matter what I did. Even my sleeping pills didn't get me any rest."

"It's because the wards are failing. She is breaking through our defenses. I didn't sleep well either, and just now when I took a shower she made the water ice cold and I could hear her laughter. I think she was coming through the mirror."

"Let's go down to the basement and see if we can force her back out. It worries me that she is gaining power. She should never have been able to make it through our wards. They are some of the strongest I've ever felt."

"Is it because she, too, was once a part of the sanctuary and its magic? Even though she has been stripped of her favor, perhaps she knows a sort of back door where she is able to sneak through?" I followed her down the stairs into the basement.

"Anything is possible. Perhaps some of the books in the attic will give us clues once we are done down here."

The door slid open as effortlessly as before, and the scene behind it still made my breath catch. The plants grew vibrant and strong, despite their lack of true sunlight. My toes dug into the rich earth and I sank to a sitting position near the burbling well as my mother pulled the door closed. She sat facing me, our knees touching. Dipping her fingers into the water, she drew symbols on my forehead, then did her own.

Dipping both her hands in once more, she grabbed mine, rubbing the droplets across the palms and back of my hands, paying special attention to the spot where my mark used to be.

"You won't know the words, so just hold my hands, keep your eyes closed and broadcast your intention to protect us, and our house and this space. The goddess will know what we seek and hopefully she will endeavor to strengthen our defenses and protect us where our own measures are failing."

My eyes drifted closed as I focused on protection. I listened to my mother's soothing voice as she chanted words in a beautiful language I didn't understand. Her voice didn't raise in volume but ratcheted up in intensity as she continued. Slipping into as near a meditative state as I found possible, I broadcast to the universe my fervent prayer for protection.

Our palms became slick against one another as she continued the mantra of our pleas for the goddess's help. Time stood still. My energy felt drained, making my body weak as we continued to beg for intervention.

Finally, her voice, which had become hoarse, began to get softer and softer. She slowed as she whispered the final words, speaking them softly and clearly. Still, I left my eyes closed until she released my hand. The sight of her face made me inhale sharply. Her skin paled and purple shadows framed her lower eyelids.

"Your face looks a whole lot like mine all of a sudden."

Her shoulders drooped, but she smiled. "I am exhausted."

"I feel like we've been here all day. Let's go back upstairs and get some food. You need the energy and I could use some too."

Closing up our secret space, I followed her closely as she climbed the stairs, somewhat afraid she might go tumbling back down. Her drop into the kitchen chair went largely ignored as I stared out the window. The sky outside was dark. Exhaustion had set in because we spent the entire day attempting to shore up our protection. No wonder my mother had nothing left in her tank.

I set about reheating some pasta from the fridge and cutting two thick slices from the homemade loaf of bread on the counter. Before she'd gotten half the bowl down, my mother's head dropped, chin to chest.

"Mom, come on. Let's get you to bed so you can rest."

She allowed me to pull her from the chair and slip her arm around my shoulders. Thankful that her bedroom was close, I helped her into bed and pulled the comforter over her. Whispering a goodnight in her ear, I pulled the bedroom door closed and left her to regain her strength.

As I cleared the table, a knock at the door startled, causing me to drop both bowls in the sink, splattering sauce across the front of me. Wearily, I pulled the curtain aside to see who could possibly be knocking. It wasn't Isaiah, come to apologize. The face on the other side of the glass belonged to Aaron.

CHAPTER THIRTEEN

Pulling the door open, I waved him in. "What are you doing here?" I whisper shouted.

He grimaced as he crossed the threshold. "I had to come see you. Weird things are happening at the pack village. I'm not sure exactly what is going on, but I didn't feel that I should stay there anymore. And why is there blood all over your porch?"

I'd forgotten about the bloody splatters. "I'm not sure where the blood came from, but I'm glad you got out of there. Have a seat. I need to finish cleaning up this mess. Are you hungry?"

His hair stood on end, as if he had static electricity running through him. The corners of his lips pursed inwards just a tiny bit and his eyebrows were drawn down. He stood stiffly in the kitchen, just barely inside the threshold. His eyes studied the floor as I studied him. Something didn't seem right, but I couldn't put my finger on it.

"No, thank you. I just came to see you because I am heading back to my own pack territory and I thought I would ask if you wanted to come with me."

"Now?" I couldn't keep the surprise from my voice. I knew I wanted to go to the other pack, but I hadn't expected it to be so soon. Or maybe suddenly was the more appropriate word.

He nodded. "Things are happening. The pack is getting stirred up and something in the reserve feels... off. I don't know what it is, but I feel like I need to get back. Now. If you don't want to come with me this time, I can try and come back for you later, but I don't know if I will be able to get here again soon."

"No, you're right. I think we need to go. Can you give me just a minute to throw some stuff into my backpack?"

I didn't wait for him to answer and hurried down the hall to my room. I threw in some spare clothes and pulled my hair into a bun. On the way out, I poked my head into my mom's room, but she still lay in bed, soundly asleep. Her chest rose and fell with deep, even breathing, and she hadn't changed position since I had gotten her into her room. Not wanting to wake her, I figured a note would have to do. That way she wouldn't be able to try and stop me since I would be long gone before she woke and realized that I left.

After a quick stop in the pantry for a couple of bottles of water and some snacks, I figured I'd gotten as ready as possible for my somewhat impromptu trip to visit another pack and meet my long-lost uncle.

"Is there anything in particular I should bring with me? Like, do I need to bring some sort of peace offering since I am meeting a new pack for the first time? Or something?"

Having no idea how packs worked, I didn't want to commit an immediate faux pas the second I stepped into their world. Whether I could technically shift or not, I didn't want to make anybody angry when the reality of it was that I needed their help. What I needed from them remained to be seen, but I had no doubt that they were meant to play an important part of our war against the evil spirit.

"No. Just come with me. I can explain things when we get there. Besides, you're not another shift venturing into their territory. You're a guest and family member to our alpha."

Something in the recesses of my brain warned me to keep my mouth shut about the little known fact that I was indeed half wolf. Since I couldn't shift at will, there didn't seem to be a reason he needed to know, and I learned more every day to trust my instincts.

A quick note jotted to my mom not to worry, that I'd be back soon, and I grabbed a handful of crackers from the package on the counter. Aaron looked at me strangely.

"For my little chipmunk friends."

He laughed. "Okay then. Ready?"

He pulled open the door and shot across the clearing into the cover of the trees, not waiting for me to lock up or place the crackers on the small table in their customary place. A glance at the sticky brown spots made me frown, but I didn't have time to clean them up now. Aaron didn't seem keen on hanging around, so I left them with a silent apology for my mother that she would have to be the one to clean them up.

"Are we in a rush? Or do you just not like my house?" I'd barely caught up to him by the treeline before he took off at a rapid pace down the trail.

"When we pass by the temple, we will be as close to their village as I wish to go. I'm hoping that if we hurry and pass by in the dead of night, there won't be any of them out to catch on to us. Are you going to tell Isaiah what you're doing?"

For a moment I argued with myself, then shook my head. "No. He kicked me out of the pack house and told me not to come back. We had a bit of an argument before I left the last time, and I think he could use a few days to cool off. He owes me an apology, and once I get one, then we'll talk about things. Maybe. I'm pretty pissed off at him at the moment."

"Do you want to talk about it?"

"Nope. Not really."

We kept a good pace as we headed toward the crumbling ruins where the spirit of my own grandmother had tried her hardest to kill me, and my exhausted body began protesting. Between my injuries, then the healing, then the energy expended to strengthen the wards of our house, I had very little left to give. A smart person would have demanded that Aaron wait for a few while I took a nap, but I guess I wasn't that smart.

We stood without speaking at the edge of the temple site once we arrived. The energy pulsated outward, rolling over us in waves. I knew she wasn't still in there, but her presence hung over the land like a shroud. Something seemed to want to pull me in, as if calling for my attention.

Scenes from the moment my mother banished her played through my head, flickering like an old-fashioned movie. What I would give to have been able to defeat her for good then, and not be racing against time to do so now. Something told me that if she managed to get her old allies back into the sanctuary, we would be facing an insurmountable foe.

Aaron reached out and touched my arm to get my attention. "We should probably keep moving. I don't want to hang out any longer than we have to. Every minute we wait, we are inviting them to catch up to us, and I don't think it would go well if they did."

Once more he turned and headed up the trail, not waiting to see if I followed. With every muscle in my body groaning, I pushed on. The further we got from the crumbling rock walls, the less drawn to the area I felt.

We made the next bit of the trek in silence, neither of us speaking until we reached the stream bed that ran through the sanctuary. The water at that particular area ran swift and deep. Despite being a good swimmer, I could never cross it in my weakened state. Nor did I want to swim in my clothes or strip down in front of Aaron.

"I know of some shallower areas around here. We can find one and wade across." He hesitated for a moment before turning and heading up the river. After a fifteen-minute walk, he stopped. "I think this is as good as we're going to find."

The water ran just as swiftly here as it had downstream, but only appeared to be shin deep. Rocks of varying sizes covered the ground below the surface, making it look slippery and treacherous in spite of the shallow depth. Not wanting to complete the journey in wet shoes, we took a moment to remove them and roll up our pant legs.

Icy shivers ran up my legs as soon as my toes dipped in at the edge. My teeth chattered before we made it halfway across, and by the time we made it to the other side, I felt like a popsicle. My hands shook as I tried to get my feet dry enough to pull my socks and shoes back on.

Crossing the stream had led us into a much denser forested part of the reserve, and very little moonlight made it through the trees. Where I had been easily able to see where I needed to put my feet before, I now stumbled over roots and rocks jutting up out of the ground. Aaron seemed to have no such problem.

"How much longer is the walk?" I felt the need to whisper, even though we were alone.

"Well, normally I would shift and run the rest of

the way as a wolf, which would only take a couple of hours. Since you can't shift, we'll be walking, and I am not really sure how long it will take us. I assume we will be there about sunrise, maybe?"

Again, little warning bells chimed, warning me to keep my secrets. I said nothing about the possibility of even trying to shift, instead apologizing for slowing him down.

"Don't worry about it. If I was in a real hurry, I wouldn't have stopped to get you."

His tone was flippant, giving me pause. Instead of calling him on it, another thought occurred to me.

"How did you know where the house was? I didn't tell you."

"What? Oh. We all know where it is. It's never been a secret, and we all knew where to find Aimee if we ever needed her for anything."

Hearing her name brought a wave of crushing grief so strong I stopped walking, almost going to my knees. My breath hitched, making it feel like drawing the air into my lungs took every bit of strength I possessed. The tear that slid down my cheek left a warm track on my chilled skin. Aaron turned around to look at me when he realized I had stopped.

"I'm sorry. I didn't mean to make you sad."

A hiccup jerked my chest, and I blew the air out noisily. "Don't be. I didn't know it would hit me that hard, just hearing her name, until it did. Every time I think I have a little control over the grief, it hits me like a freight train. Sometimes over the most inconsequential things."

"I feel that way about the loss of my mom. She died a few years ago, and every time I think I am finally accepting that she is gone, something dumb comes along and I lose it again."

Pain made his voice quiver. The darkness made it all but impossible to see his face, and yet I felt his sorrow in my very bones. It rolled out from him like thunder.

With a deep breath, he pulled it back in, leashing it once more and stuffing it into whatever hiding place he had created for his weakness. Not wanting to pry, I didn't ask any questions, just offered my apology.

"It's okay. I wouldn't have told you if I didn't want to. I just wanted you to know that I understand.

We didn't have as much contact with your aunt as the other pack did, but everybody loved her."

"Everyone but her own mother." A wind whipped around us as I made the statement. "I don't know why I said that. I'm just so angry that I am related to this evil thing that killed her own daughter, and tried her hardest to kill her granddaughter. How did we come from something so rotten?"

"Perhaps she wasn't always evil?"

His notion brought memories back to me of the way my own mom had spoken of her mother as I grew up. All the signs evident that something about our family hadn't been exactly "normal." And yet never in my wildest dreams would I have suspected the truth of the situation. In spite of that, I found myself here, stumbling along after a virtual stranger, in the dead of night, toward an unknown destination to meet an uncle that had been missing my entire life.

Any semblance of a trail had long since disappeared, and I followed Aaron through the trees as he wound around them. Praying he knew where he was going, I plodded along after him, cussing as I tripped over the obstacles hidden by the darkness. My body ached and my brain shut down all but the most necessary processes.

It became easier to see as the night loosened its stranglehold on the scenery around us while we walked. Conversation had mostly ceased when I quit being able to formulate any articulate sentences. The sun began to tinge the sky pink when Aaron finally told me we didn't have much farther to go. Nerves cramped my stomach. All of a sudden, I had doubts about my decision. Even though Aaron said my uncle knew about me, way more than I knew about him, I questioned whether I should have come at all.

Instinct told me when we arrived, even though I saw nothing to give it away at first. As we walked, I felt someone watching us. Aaron gave me a reassuring smile.

"It's okay. We're here. Don't be worried."

I tried to smile, but even my facial muscles were in rebellion. None of my body parts wanted to work right, and I didn't know how much longer I could stay awake. The last thing I wanted to do was introduce myself to Rick and then ask for a place to take a nap. Talk about embarrassing. What an excellent first impression that would make.

We rounded an outcropping of rocks, and I found myself staring at a small village. Small cabins, similar to those in Isaiah's territory, dotted the clearing. Cliffs rose along two of the sides. My tired brain couldn't catalog all the details before my eyes came to rest on a figure standing in the center of a clearing.

In my heart, I knew that was Rick. My uncle. Aimee's husband. The man I hoped could help me, or at least provide some answers. He began walking our way as we moved further out of the forest.

Rick's hands reached out to grab mine. "Leah. Welcome."

Before I could respond, our hands joined. A jolt of electricity shot up my arms and numbness spread throughout my body. My body gave out without letting me utter a single word, and blackness took over.

CHAPTER FOURTEEN

My eyelids fluttered as I attempted to recognize the faces hanging over me when I came to. Slowly, Aaron's face came into focus above me. I struggled to sit up and felt gentle hands pushing against my shoulders.

My uncle Rick's voice came to me from the side. "Don't try to get up just yet. Give yourself a minute to get oriented."

How embarrassing! I closed my eyes again in an attempt to hide for myself.

Aaron and Rick chuckled together. "Don't be embarrassed," Aaron said. "You've been through an awful lot lately."

I grimaced and let them know I was ready to sit up. "Laying here on the dirt in the middle of your villages aren't going to change that. I can at least get up and maintain some sense of dignity."

Each of them took one hand and helped me to my feet. The world swayed around me for a minute before steadying. I could see others from the pack off to the side, standing back far enough to give me some room, but close enough to keep an eye on the newcomer. Their curiosity hung in the air.

"How about we take this inside, where I can get you something to drink and you can rest? There is more than enough time to introduce you to the rest of the pack in a little while." Uncle Rick took my arm and led me towards the cabin situated directly in the center of the village. Aaron followed along.

Despite the headache that was worming its way through my skull, I needed answers. More than I needed sleep, more than I needed anything else at that moment. My only desire was to hear Rick's story from start to finish, and learn as much about the past as I could.

Upon entering the cabin, he seated me at a small, round table, offering me the options of tea or coffee. I grinned at him. "Coffee please. I am in desperate need of the caffeine."

"I assume you still take French vanilla creamer and sugar, no?"

Surprised that he knew the way I took my coffee, I simply nodded. I hadn't realized how cold my hands were until I wrapped them around the warm mug as he handed it to me. "Thank you."

"Of course. It's the least I can do to get you settled until we are ready to have a more in-depth conversation. I assume you have a lot of questions."

My laughter snorted out before I could keep control of it. "That's an understatement!"

"Would you like to get started now, or would you rather nap first? You seem like you could use the rest."

"I'm exhausted, mentally and physically, but I really want to drink my coffee, so could we talk while I do that?"

"Absolutely. Where do you want to start?"

"I guess with whatever you think is most important for me to know now. I'm so lost, but I'm not really sure which direction I should be going in."

"You have a lot on your plate. I don't envy you."

"It seems like despite all my best efforts, I can't seem to do what needs to be done." Not caring that Aaron sat next to me, I held my hand out to him, my bare palm aching in shame. "I lost my mark. All because I was stupid."

Rick shook his head. "You're not stupid. Considering the amount of time you've had to wrap your head around the situation here, I'd say you've done a damn good job. You can't blame yourself for the things you didn't know."

"Oh no. I blame my mother for that. I can't help but think that if I had grown up my whole life knowing about my heritage, that I would've mastered most of my magic long before this happened and we may never have gotten to this place. Now I'm doing my best to play catch-up. And I think I'm sucking at it."

He reached out and touched my arm. "I know

you're angry with your mother, but I do believe she had your best interests at heart. I don't think that anyone ever expected us to get to this place."

"It still wasn't her right! Sometimes, part of me is mad at Aimee too, for not telling me. I feel like she may have intended to tell me as I grew into adulthood, and then life just got in the way. I didn't make it out to see her again, and the guilt is eating me alive. I know that part of this is my fault too, no matter how badly I wish it wasn't."

Rick sighed. I could hear him blowing out the excess air as he gathered his thoughts. "There is so much you don't know. I can fill you in on a lot of it, but I want you to know ahead of time that some of it is going to be painful to hear. I just want you to keep in mind that nobody did this to be hurtful, in spite of how it might seem."

Our eyes met, and I became worried at the pained expression on his face. Something told me this wasn't going to be the happy homecoming of blissful stories that I could somehow hope it would be. I was about to get an education in the past and the present. That was going to be hard to swallow.

Lifting my mug to my lips, I was surprised to find it cold and now empty. My hands shook as I set it back down on a table with a thump. Part of me wanted to ask him to refill it so that I didn't have to start in on what I knew was going to be a difficult conversation. The other part of me was so exhausted, all I wanted to do was find a horizontal surface and close my eyes. Rick took the decision-making out of my hands.

"How about I get you settled in my guest room, and you can take a nap? I have a feeling that much of this will be easier to swallow when you are rested."

Unable to make my tongue in my brain work together, I nodded, standing up. He showed me the way to the spare room, pointing out the bathroom along the way.

"Make yourself comfortable and get some rest. I won't go far, so head on out when you awake."

"Thank you so much." I kicked off my shoes, slid into the bed and didn't have another conscious thought before drifting off into sleep. For the first time in a long while, the sleep I slept felt restful and restorative.

Sunlight shone through the windows the next

time I opened my eyes. I stretched without sitting up, not quite ready to give up my nap.

Even the promise of getting the answers I sought was not enough to drive me from my pillow. I'd been waiting all this time. What was a few more minutes? Before I knew it, my eyes drifted closed, and I was asleep again. This nap, however, was not so restful.

Mist swirled around me as I stood in the now familiar clearing of my dreams. There was no sound, and I saw no other living being. Shivers wracked my body, and I couldn't be sure if it was from the chill or the fear that I felt building. As always, when in the dreamscape, I couldn't be sure if I should be quiet and hiding, or if I should call out to see if someone else was there.

Heavy footsteps reached my ears. I spun in a circle, looking for their origin. If something or someone else was there, the mist hid them from my sight. My eyes strained, and my ears remained on alert. Glimpses of a figure shone through the mist so quickly I couldn't be sure if they were really there before they were gone again. It seemed as if someone, or something, was circling me.

My desire to see who was in the dreamscape with me outweighed my fear of whatever I was about to run into. Was it Isaiah? And if so, what was he doing here? A brief parting of the mist showed me a person, tall and dark-haired. I didn't recognize them. At least, I didn't think so.

"Hello?"

Silence met my inquiry. Whoever it was, they weren't interested in having a conversation. They never came any closer, never spoke to me, and disappeared back into the mist, leaving me alone.

"Leah! Leah!"

I opened my eyes to see Rick standing above the bed. Worry was written across his face. I shook my head to clear the last vestiges of the dream and rolled onto my side. His warm hand reached out and covered one of my freezing ones.

"Are you okay?"

"I was having one of my strange dreams again."

"Can you tell me about it? I could feel the magic rolling off you in waves, and I was becoming afraid I wouldn't be able to wake you up."

"There's not much to tell. I'm standing in a

clearing, usually alone, and there is a white mist swirling about me everywhere. It's always cold, and very rarely is there anyone else there. Sometimes I never even hear a sound. This time I could hear someone walking around me, but only got a glimpse of them. A taller dark-haired man was there, and then he was gone again. The next thing I knew; I was waking up."

"I'm afraid the evil spirit has found a way to reach you in your dreams. This is not a good thing. Here, of all places, you should be protected even from her."

"Why? Why is this place special?"

"If you're ready, how about you get up and get yourself refreshed? Come on out when you're done, and I will start from the beginning. It's going to be a long story, but it's one I think you need to hear."

Being faced with the possibility of getting answers to all the questions I had been asking gave me a sudden case of cold feet. I took a little longer than necessary to join him in the dining room. My desire to have the knowledge, warred with my fear of what I was about to hear. He'd warned me it was going to be difficult, so I knew all the things I was about to learn weren't going to be pleasant.

Making a detour into the washroom, I splashed cold water on my face. Staring into the mirror, I searched my own eyes, wondering if I was ready for what was about to be revealed to me. It wasn't as if I had much choice. I'd been asking for answers, and I was about to get them, whether I liked them or not.

Unease curled my toes. I didn't like the fact that he thought I should be safe from the evil spirit here, and yet she'd slipped into my dreams as easily as coming through an unlocked door. Was there anywhere I would be safe? Anywhere she couldn't get to me?

The realization that the answer to that question was probably not steeled my resolve to be rid of her once and for all. I owed Aimee at least that much. And if the answers Rick was about to give me were pieces to that puzzle, I wanted them no matter how badly they hurt.

His eyes met mine as I entered the room. "I took the liberty of making you another cup of coffee to tide you over until I knew what you wanted to eat. You must be starving."

Just as I was about to tell him I'd rather have answers than food, my stomach grumbled loudly. I laughed out loud. "I'm not picky. Whatever you have handy is fine with me."

"How about something quick? I heard your stomach!"

"I won't argue with you there, since my biology has betrayed me already."

He turned around and began rooting in the refrigerator. He popped his head back up over the door and lifted a pot with a lid. "Soup okay? One of the pack members made it yesterday. It's delicious, and quick to heat up."

"That sounds delightful. For some reason, I seem to not realize how hungry I am until food becomes an option. Then I'm ravenous."

He chuckled. "This will just take a moment. Drink your coffee and food will be on the table momentarily."

I watched him as he worked, trying to take in everything about him. This man was my uncle. He'd been married to my aunt Aimee, in spite of the fact that he hadn't been around. He was family. Part of me wondered what it would've been like if he'd been in the picture as I visited aunt Aimee. Would I have guessed about their secret life?

His motions were smooth and precise, wasting no energy unnecessarily. He seemed to be very comfortable having me sitting at his dining room table. If he was nervous about the conversation we were about to have, he didn't show it.

The smells wafting from the pot made my mouth water. Thankfully he was true to his word, and before I knew it he was scooping the soup into a pair of matching bowls and joining me at the chair across the table. I suddenly wondered if I'd be able to eat and have a conversation at the same time.

"Do you want to eat before we begin?" He asked me the question gently, almost as if he could read my reservations.

Deciding to be as noncommittal as possible, I shrugged. "It might be easier to talk if we don't have food in our mouths?"

He nodded, and we ate in silence. The soup was delicious, and calming in a way I hadn't expected.

Something about it made me feel ready to hear what he had to say, no matter what it turned out to be. Or perhaps it wasn't the soup, it was simply the realization that I didn't have any other choices.

His spoon clanked into an empty bowl. "I'll start while you finish eating. Let me know if you decide you want more. Is there anywhere in particular you'd like me to begin?"

"I suppose at the very beginning would be the best place."

"I'm sure you wonder why you never saw me when you went to visit Aimee."

I looked at him in surprise. "No," I drew the word out slowly. "She and my mom both told me about how you disappeared. I knew you existed, and that Aimee was heartbroken to have lost you."

He looked at me steadily and took a deep breath. "I was never lost. I saw Aimee as often as I could. It wasn't enough, but it was all we had."

The spoon slipped from my grasp as I stared at him in shock. Aimee had lied to me all those years?

CHAPTER FIFTEEN

The spoon sent splatters of soup flying in all directions. My mouth hung open and my eyebrows shot up to my hairline. Ugly, rolling waves of shock ripped through me, threatening to bring the soup and coffee right back up to the tabletop.

"Excuse me?"

Thoughts rolled through my head so fast that I barely had a chance to knowledge them before the next one crowded its way in. Everything I thought I knew to be true about Aimee's life had been a lie.

Perhaps not everything, but so many of the most important things. For all of my life growing up, I had believed Aimee to be one of my closest confidants.

While I didn't expect her to spill all the aspects of her personal life to me as a child, I certainly believed that as I grew older, I deserved at least some of the truth from her. Why had she continued to hide it from me? The physical pain this revelation brought to my chest was unbearable.

"Leah, please don't be mad at Amy. She wanted so badly to tell you."

"Then why didn't she?" I couldn't control the raising of my voice, and before I had finished the sentence, I was standing.

"I know you're hurt. And I don't expect you to understand everything right away. But please sit down and at least listen to her side of the story, as best that I can tell it to you. There was a reason."

My fingertips dug into the edge of the tabletop, trembling as I tried to decide if I wanted to sit down and listen to him or run out that front door and not come back. Who else had been lying to me my entire life? Had my mother known about this, too?

Rick sat silently, watching me and waiting. He was respectful of my silence and gave me a minute to collect myself. Thankfully, he didn't speak, because I think any other words would've driven me right out of the cabin.

Tears began to fall as I sucked in a deep breath, and then another, before hiding my face behind my hands and letting it all out. My whole body shook with sobs, and every time I tried to take a deep breath, I felt like an elephant was trampling my chest. My throat burned. My head throbbed. My legs gave out, and I plopped back into the chair with zero grace.

"Why? I don't understand why there had to be all the lies."

Rick gave me a moment to compose myself before trying to answer my question. I think he knew it was a rhetorical one, because even in my grief, I knew he wouldn't have all the answers. Only Aimee herself could've told me exactly why she made the choices she did. Unfortunately, I no longer had the opportunity to ask her about them.

I felt a hand towel pressed up against the back of my hands and took it to try and wipe my face. Luckily,

I had pretty much given up wearing any makeup, or the mess made of my mascara would have turned me into a raccoon. It was bad enough I was getting snot all over his kitchen towel. At that moment, I was too hurt to be embarrassed.

"Aimee was the love of my life. And even though I knew it would be safest for her, I couldn't walk away from her completely. I don't know how much you know about the story of your grandmother's death, or many of the things that happened when you were a child. All I can tell you are the things I know for certain, and you are more than welcome to go back and ask your mother for clarification."

"Did my mother know you and Aimee were still in contact?" To me, she had seemed to be totally certain that my aunt was a grieving new wife who lost her husband. After all the other lies she told me, though, I didn't know what to believe.

"I can't say for certain, but I don't believe she did. Aimee and I agreed that if anyone other than us knew, it would become infinitely more dangerous for us to see each other. We already knew, at that time, that your grandmother's spirit was the one wreaking havoc. We hoped that by not allowing her to know that we were working together, we might get the upper hand. I'm not sure how successful we were."

Expressions flickered across his face so quickly that I barely had time to identify them before they were gone. Something in his voice made me want to believe every word he said. After all the lies I believed, I planned on taking everything with a grain of salt.

"Time is of the essence, so I'm going to make the story as short as possible while still making sure you get the necessary details. Later on, I am more than open to answering any questions you have. We knew from the time your mother got pregnant that you would most likely be bestowed the gift of the mark. To be perfectly honest, I was shocked you weren't born with it."

"I thought you and aunt Aimee didn't meet until I was a child?"

"We didn't get to know each other well until then. But I knew her. I also knew your grandmother, your mother, and most of the other residents of the sanctuary."

All of a sudden, I jerked upright. "Do you know my father?"

Rick paused, pressing his lips together. "In order to be totally transparent, I have to tell you that I do not know for a fact who your father is. I do have my suspicions, but I would prefer you ask your mother for that information. I do not want to give you the wrong answers. If it comes to the point that she refuses to tell you anything at all, I will give you what pieces I do know and try to help you find out for sure."

As much as I wanted to know of my parentage, I didn't think it would be helpful in beating the evil spirit, which meant that I had to push it to the side for now. There would be time in the future to get it figured out. Now was not the time to let myself become distracted. I had too many other things to learn.

"Aimee and I agreed I needed to be here, in this village, and this part of the sanctuary, for a very good reason, which I will show you when we are done having our conversation here. I snuck away as often as possible to visit her. Sometimes, I hid in the treeline to watch the two of you. I felt it was the closest I could come to protecting you while you were here at the sanctuary. At that time, many of us were still stronger than your grandmother."

"My mother told me she got stronger by making unclean deals with outsiders. Is that true?"

"In some ways, yes. She had been practicing her magic for a long time and researching ways to increase her strength. The deals she made with those from the outside were only one avenue she explored."

"Do you know why? Was she always evil?" The fear that I was tainted with her evil by my very ancestry settled in the pit of my stomach. What if she had passed down some of it to me? I can picture it hiding inside of me, waiting for its opportunity to rise up and take over.

"Again, I can't say for certain. None of us really has the power to see inside another. Sometimes, though, having a great amount of power simply makes one greedy for more. It blinds them. There becomes a point in time where it overtakes them, and then the only thing that matters is getting more. It's like a drug. It ruins families, communities, and even those we wouldn't necessarily think of as evil can fall prey to it."

Sadness for her crept up. Perhaps at one point she had been a loving mother. I mourned the loss of my chance to have a real grandmother, the kind that would have baked cookies with me and told me stories.

"When she cast a spell on the creek and began the curse, I knew we would be safe here. The magic that protects us is, so far, stronger than anything your grandmother could muster. That is part of the reason I was so surprised to feel the magic rolling off you from your dream. She shouldn't be able to reach you here. She is getting stronger and we need to hurry."

"What is it that protects this place so strongly? Is it that there are so many people with strong magic living here?"

He pushed his chair back and stood. "How about if we take a walk, so that I can show you? I will explain on the way."

He waited until I stood before turning and leaving through the front door. The eyes from the other members of the pack followed us, but nobody attempted to join us. I couldn't help but wonder what they knew of me, and what they thought of me. Did they all know I had lost my mark? Were they ashamed of me? They loved Aimee so much. I knew I had big shoes to follow. I also knew that it was unlikely I could ever fill them.

We walked along the trail back into the woods and climbed up as it wound around the cliff. Flowers lined the pathway. In spite of being an emotional mess, something about the walk soothed my worries. Rick continued his story as we moved forward, pausing every so often to see if I had any questions. So far, I hadn't gotten the feeling that he was lying to me.

Turning a corner, we came upon a jumbled thicket of vines hanging from the cliff wall. Pushing through them, Rick led me into a large cavern. Stopping short, I couldn't help but stare. Crystals randomly jutted from the walls. A gorgeous blue pool burbled in the back corner. In the center, a giant stone altar stood. Its surface was covered in runes and symbols I did not recognize.

"What is this place?"

Rick held out his arms to encompass the cavern. "This is our connection to the very magic that powers this reserve. This altar allows us to connect with the magic of our goddess. It allows us to receive our blessings."

Moments passed as I stared at it in shock. I had no idea such a thing existed. For some reason, it never occurred to me that the essence of the sanctuary was tied to a physical object. For some reason, I had assumed it was tied to the magic of its people.

Even after seeing the crumbling temple on the other side of the reserve, it hadn't crossed my mind. Those ruins had seemed to me to be more like a church. A place they went to honor the goddess, not necessarily receive magic from her.

"Because our magic is bestowed upon us by the goddess, it only remains strong as long as we, the people of the sanctuary, are loyal to her. The Western pack, the one Isaiah is now alpha of, betrayed that loyalty. Without their help, the evil spirit would never have been able to bring in outsiders. She never would've gained power from them, and never would have become strong enough to overthrow us."

Even as angry as Isaiah had made me, my first instinct was to defend him. "You don't understand! Isaiah is not like that. He is loyal to the sanctuary, and not the whole reason he removed their previous alpha."

"I don't believe Isaiah is evil. Unfortunately, I also don't believe he is strong enough to maintain his lead over that pack. Not at this time. There are too many that live there who still wish to see the outsiders return. The power they bring with them is too great of a temptation. What they also do not understand, however, is that that power will not flow to them with their arrival. It will overtake them and turn them into slaves. Just so you know, while you were napping, I sent Aaron back to the other pack. My hope is that he will learn new information to bring back to us."

A small spark of hope bloomed in my chest, completely overriding the part about Aaron returning to Isaiah's pack. "Is this altar capable of returning my mark to me? Is this where I come to regain the goddess's favor?"

"While I cannot guarantee that the goddess will return her favor to you, I do believe she will. It will not be easy, but I know someone who can help. I will admit that I was shocked to feel you pull your wolf forward, even missing your connection to the sanctuary."

"It took just about everything I had, and I almost wasn't sure I'd survive it. My mom had to force the change and then force it back. How did you know? I never left the house."

"I assume the change took place in the special room in the basement?" When I nodded, he continued. "I thought so, because I felt nothing, and then all of a sudden, your wolf was there. The second you stepped over the threshold, I was able to sense you. I knew when you disappeared from my consciousness that you had gone back into the room. I never felt your wolf again, so I assume that was where you changed back as well."

His admission made me worry. "Does that mean the evil spirit is aware that I was able to change forms?"

"Most likely. However, she is also aware that

without your mark, you cannot willingly change forms without help."

"So, if I had my mark again, I would be able to change back and forth at will?" The prospect both excited and terrified me.

"Yes."

"How can I earn my mark back? I will do anything. I had magic for a very little amount of time, but I feel so broken without it. It was like being made whole, only to be shattered into a million pieces soon after."

"I don't have the power to help you, but there is someone in the village who can. I'd like to take you back and introduce the two of you, if you're up for it?"

"What are we waiting for?" I took a last glance at the altar before turning back toward the entrance.

As we made our way back toward the village, Rick continued to answer my questions as best he could. The short amount of time was nowhere near enough for me to learn everything I needed, but I felt like I was getting a good start. Hopefully, I would be able to get enough answers before the evil spirit decided to attack. I needed my mark back.

CHAPTER SIXTEEN

This time, as we walked through the small village, Rick took the time to begin introducing me to those we passed on our way. Try as I did, I knew there was no way I would remember all of their names, and admitted that I'd have to ask again the next time we met.

"Hello." A tall woman with long dark hair walked up to Rick and me, once the crowd had dispersed a little.

Rick turned to face her. Gesturing my way, he

introduced us. "Ophelia, this is Leah, Aimee's niece. Leah, this is Ophelia."

She extended both hands and grasped one of mine between them. As our skin made contact, I felt a chill fall over me. She had powerful magic. With determination, I managed to not pull my hand from hers.

"Leah, it's a pleasure to meet you." She smiled, revealing perfect white teeth.

"Hello, I'm glad to meet you too. My uncle says that you could possibly help me restore my magic? I assume at this point you know that I have lost the mark, and things are not going so well."

She let out a little chuckle. "I'm glad you're not one to waste words, and there's no time like the present to get started. I can try to restore your magic, but there are no guarantees. It's going to be a fairly difficult process, but I believe we have a chance. We will need to prepare a ritual that will once more tie your powers to the magic of the reserve."

"All I need to know is what to do. There's nothing I wouldn't do to get my magic back. This borrowed magic of my mother's isn't the same."

"There is one caveat," Ophelia cautioned. "If we tie your powers to the land of this reserve, they will only work here. You will not have any powers outside of the lands governed by the goddess."

"It's certainly better than having no magic at all. Without getting something back, I have no chance at defeating the evil spirit."

While the thought of losing my magic outside of the reserve made me sad, I would take it over having no magic at all, anywhere. Here on the reserve is where I needed it the most. Without it, we would never defeat my grandmother, and having magic anywhere else would no longer matter.

Ophelia told Rick and me that she needed to gather a few things for the ritual, and she would meet us at the cave in about an hour. Before we can turn back toward the trail, a young man comes running from the forest.

"Alpha. Our concerns were valid. The alpha of the Western pack has been overtaken. He is no longer in charge, and members of that pack are mobilizing to do something they are being very sneaky about!"

Rick thanked him and sent him on his way. At my

sharp intake of breath, he turned to me, resting his hand on my shoulder. "Try not to worry."

My legs felt weak. Had Isaiah been injured? I looked at Rick. "You don't think they killed him, do you? Do you think he is injured?"

He shook his head. "If they had killed him, I would've been told. I can't, however, guarantee that he was not injured in the fight for the position."

The need to see him bubbled up inside of me. As badly as I wanted to restore my magic, I needed to know that he was okay. Everything I had been angry about just a little bit ago seemed inconsequential and small.

Before I could utter a word, Rick seem to know what I was going to say. "We cannot go to him now. It would start an all-out war. A war that we are not prepared to fight yet. We need to get your magic restored and then worry about the other pack."

As much as I hated to admit it, he made sense. Without my magic, I was as good as useless, and I couldn't go picking fights that I was guaranteed not to win. Nor could I bring the fight to the doorstep of this pack. I needed to worry about the most important things first, and then I would see how we could help Isaiah. I just prayed to the goddess he wasn't injured too badly.

Ophelia returned to the clearing before Rick and I even got headed up the path to the cave. Apparently, we had been standing there talking for longer than I realized, or she was quicker getting her things together than she thought she would be. In her hand, she carried a black velvet bag and nothing more.

Together, we headed up the trail back to the altar. Ophelia gave me a quick run over of what would be required of me, and what I could expect during the ritual. She let me know that Rick would have to wait outside, and after she performed the beginning of the ritual, I would be alone with the altar to finish it. Nerves crawled up my spine. What if the goddess found me unworthy? Again?

Ophelia was the one to reach the vines first, sweeping them aside and stepping into the cave. She stopped in her tracks, inhaling sharply as Rick and I bumped into her. Tears filled my eyes as I peered past her into the cave. Its beauty from just a short time before had been destroyed. The altar itself lay in multiple pieces on the floor of the cavern.

"How could this have happened?" Rick and I both looked at Ophelia.

She shook her head. "I do not know. Whatever destroyed the altar is a powerful being indeed."

"Can you still perform the ritual?" As badly as I wanted her to say yes, I knew in my heart that the answer would be negative.

"I'm sorry. I can't. The magic of the altar is what is needed to tie your powers to the reserve once more. Without it, there is nothing to anchor the spell."

Rick's gaze swept over the damage. "Why wouldn't the reserve protect itself? I don't understand how it allowed this to happen."

Ophelia glanced at me before turning back to Rick. "While I can't be certain, I believe it is because of the lack of a witch to hold the mark. As long as there is a potential candidate, the reserve can maintain its strength. The power would remain intact, waiting." She turned to look at me once more. "I am afraid the goddess did not find you worthy to hold the mark any longer."

Before I could shout at her, Rick intervened.

"That isn't necessarily the case. It could simply be that the magic came along was more intense than the altar could resist. Either way, we need to find a new way to restore your magic."

"I don't understand! I did the best I could with the information I had at the time! How can the goddess punish me for trying to do what I could to help? If it was so important for me to do things a certain way, why didn't the goddess show me that way?"

"I cannot answer that. My magic does not come from the goddess." Ophelia shrugged.

Rick looked lost. "I cannot answer what the goddess chooses to do. We may never know her reasons, but that doesn't mean we should give up."

"I've had it! I've had it with the high and mighty goddess. I've had it with my stupid grandmother who decided to be evil, and I have had it with magic! Since I can't seem to do anything right, maybe I don't need to be here at all."

I could hear Rick and Ophelia calling my name as I spun on my heel and stormed out of the cave. Refusing to turn back and look at them, I dashed off down the trail. Fear and anger drove my feet forward, and my brain took very little part in deciding which way we went.

Taking a small side path, I found my way to the bank of the stream. Brushing the leaves off a fallen log, I sat and watched the water burble among the rocks. Eyes closed, I let the tears leak out. The frustration was getting to me. As much as I wanted to throw my hands up and run away, I knew I couldn't. I'd never forgive myself if I did.

Kicking off my shoes and socks, I buried my feet in the dirt. I reached out with every fiber of my being, hoping to reconnect with the goddess of the land. My heart implored her to give me another chance.

Rolling up my pant legs, I walked to the edge of the water. Dipping my toes in, I shivered at the cold. My eyes marveled in its clarity, a reminder that it came from the pristine source in the mountain above me. Blessed water, because the goddess wished it so. I stood in it until my feet were numb, then returned to my log. The forest remained quiet around me, and I found myself wondering about my chipmunk friends.

Thoughts of Aimee pushed their way to the

forefront. The one person I believed I could always trust, and she lied to me my entire life. The opportunity for closure would never come, because she was already gone. Even though the thought made my heart ache, I knew I had to bring that closure to myself. If I didn't, it would eat me up inside. The last thing I wanted was for my emotions to cause me to make another mistake. Nobody could afford for me to screw up again.

Rick lowered himself onto the log beside me, startling me. "I didn't even hear you coming!"

"I'm sorry. I wasn't trying to sneak up on you. I just wanted to check in and see how you were doing."

"I don't know. It's so hard to reconcile the things my brain knows with the emotions my heart feels. I'm sad and scared and stressed and mad all at the same time. The pressure to do the right thing feels like it's crushing me sometimes."

"Leadership can be like that sometimes," Rick said gently.

"But I'm not a leader. I am the least experienced person of the bunch, and I feel like I'm running around trying to play catch-up. Unsuccessfully, I might add. I very likely have lost the possibility of having my magic back at all, and yet I still need to find a way to defeat the evil spirit. I'm quite literally on a mission to kill my own grandmother."

"Ophelia is working on some options for us. She is going to do her best to help you. She will make one attempt to restore the altar, although she doesn't believe she will be successful and I tend to agree with her. Ophelia is a powerful witch in her own right, but she is not beholden to our goddess, nor is she an original resident of this land."

"I appreciate that she's willing to try, and I'm sorry I acted like a child earlier. You'd think I was twelve years old again."

"To be fair, you have endured a lot of trauma recently, both physical and emotional. Cut yourself some slack. We all know you're doing the best that you can, and you have already made incredible progress. Nobody else was able to break the curse on the stream that the dark spirit set. You, and you alone, returned the ability to shift to the Western pack. That's pretty impressive."

"But was it the wrong choice? It's how I lost my

mark to begin with."

Rick patted my knee and stood up. "I think rather than questioning whether our choices are right or wrong, sometimes we are better served by asking if we believe we did the right thing at the time. We all make mistakes, and we all move on. When you get hungry, come back to the cabin and we'll eat. For now, I'll leave you here with your thoughts."

His words hung in the air between us. They were a reminder that I truly believed I was doing the right thing at the time. Even if I had made a mistake, my intentions were pure. I wanted nothing more than to do the best I could for the residents of the sanctuary. I wanted to make Aunt Aimee proud, in spite of being angry about the lies. Deep inside, I knew she had only told them because she felt she had to. Once again, it was an example of someone doing what they believed was right at the time.

Leaves crunched, and a stick broke in the woods to my side. Thinking Rick had returned, I turned in the direction of the sound. For a moment, I saw nothing. A chill crept up my spine. All of a sudden, the deepening twilight seemed more menacing than it had a moment before. Darkness could hide many things.

"Leah?"

I jumped to my feet in shock as Isaiah made his way out of the bushes. "What are you doing here?"

"I've been looking for you everywhere! I'm sorry we argued." He reached out and grabbed my hand.

My eyes took in the fading bruises covering his face. "What happened to you?" A small part of me wondered if he was going to tell me the truth.

"Don't worry about this," he gestured with his other hand. "I heal quickly. We have a bigger problem."

"What is it?"

"Aaron returned to my pack. He incited some of the other members to challenge me for my alpha status. It was three against one, and I lost. I managed to fend them off and get out of there before they killed me, and I have been looking for you ever since. I could tell you weren't at your house, but it was very hard to sense you over here."

"So much has been going on! I need to introduce you to my uncle Rick. And he needs to know what

Aaron has done."

Before I could lead him back to the village, Rick returned with a number of pack members in tow. With an apologetic look my way, he asked them to escort Isaiah back to the clearing. Why did he need an escort? Did he really think Isaiah was here to cause trouble?

CHAPTER SEVENTEEN

Rick sent Isaiah on ahead with the other members of the pack, putting his hand on my shoulder to hold me back. Pulling away from him, I kept watch on Isaiah until I could see him no more. "Why is he a prisoner?"

"He is not a prisoner. However, we need to be extra careful right now. We need to be sure that he is not under the influence of any other magic."

Recognizing the need for caution, I nodded and began to follow them up the trail. As we walked, Rick explained to me what he planned to do when we got back to the village. "Isaiah likely has information that will prove valuable. We just need to talk to him to get it."

"I know he'll do whatever he can to help us. He said Aaron was the one who encouraged them to challenge him."

Rick's brows drew together, but he didn't respond. As we returned to the clearing, Rick led me to a small building on the edge of the forest. Inside, I saw Isaiah sitting on a chair, with the pack members standing around him. He still maintained his alpha demeanor and looked sure and steady as he sat amongst them. Guilt for running off on him flooded me.

Walking up to stand next to him, I introduced him to Rick. Rick asked for a couple more chairs, and the two of us sat down with Isaiah. The pack members faded to the back, but didn't leave the building.

Time flew by as Isaiah explained what had been happening since I'd left. Rick and I both answered questions as well as asked them. Between the three of us, we seemed to get a good timeline of what happened, and some idea of what the other pack's plans were. The members who had challenged Isaiah were ones who'd been in league with the evil spirit before, just like the previous alpha.

"If Aaron truly is responsible for this, something needs to be done about him."

Rick looked chagrined. "He has been acting off lately, but he has been somewhat strange since his mother passed away anyways. While I noticed the change, it didn't seem threatening at the time."

"Do you think it's possible he's under the evil spirit influence? That he is been bribed or coerced to do these things?"

"It certainly wouldn't be outside the scope of her power."

Rick and Isaiah had a brief conversation about the series of events leading up to Aaron appearing in our pack for the first time. At that point in time, Rick had had no idea he was going to make his way across the peninsula to those lands. He just up and disappeared one day.

Isaiah and I then filled Rick in on what had happened while Aaron was staying with the Western pack. I told him all about how Aaron had been the one to inform me he lived here, and that Aunt Aimee likely hadn't been a widow after all.

Rick explained to Isaiah that he had sent Aaron back solely to keep eyes on the pack, that he'd had no intention of toppling him from his position as alpha. After the rumors had begun swirling about the outside influences possibly returning to the reserve, he'd wanted an inside guy to keep an eye on things.

"I apologize I made the wrong decision about who to send."

Isaiah accepted his apology. "None of us could have known what the evil spirit would do next. The sooner we get Leah's magic back and can defeat her, the better for all of us. We need to get this under control before somebody else gets hurt."

"Perhaps my mother can come here, and she can show me how to use her magic. She wanted to show me before, but I declined. Now more than ever, I need magic of any sort."

"At this point, I say we do anything we can, although your mother may not wish to come here. Either way, Aaron needs to be stopped, especially if he is under the evil spirit's influence. The more time the other pack has to do their dirty work, the harder it will be to overcome them. In this case, I will not argue about you using the magic not of the reserve."

Rick asked one of the pack members to fetch Ophelia for him. He and Isaiah continued to talk as we waited, while I sat in my chair quietly mulling over my options. The goddess had made it apparent she did not wish to restore my mark, so I would find my magic elsewhere. Without it, I was nothing.

The last thing I wanted was to face my grandmother's evil spirit with no way to defend myself and no way to put her in her place. Whatever it took for me to overcome her, I was willing to do. This had to end before it was too late. I couldn't bear to let her take anyone else from me.

Ophelia made her way through the front door and through the pack members. "You needed me?"

"Yes, thank you for coming. After much discussion, we have decided that we need Leah to have access to magic. Do you have a way to help her learn to access it?"

Ophelia frowned. "Do you realize that if we take this route, the goddess may never return your mark?

Some actions are seen as irredeemable, and this may very well be one of them."

"I understand. But I don't feel like I have any other choice. In order to beat the evil spirit, I have to fight magic with magic. I can't do that if I don't have any. For me to wait and hope that the goddess restores my mark means I would be endangering everyone who lives here. I'd be endangering everyone who lives outside of the sanctuary as well. I don't think that would be a fair choice for me to make."

Isaiah reached out and grabbed my hand. "If it makes you feel any better, I'm behind you one hundred percent. I'll do whatever I can to help. You're right when you say that our choices here will affect everyone. I owe my pack this much, at least."

Ophelia's eyes flicked to Rick. He inclined his head towards her, letting him know he was onboard to move forward. Her dark eyes pierced mine as she studied my face. It felt like she was trying to read my soul. Instead of shrinking back, as I might've done before, I met her gaze head-on. She needed to see that I was serious.

"Give me fifteen minutes to gather my things and

meet me at the waterfall." She glanced Rick's way as if to ensure he would take us. With his nod, she turned and walked back out the door.

The weight of what was about to happen settled over me in the silence of the hall. The pack members lining the room didn't speak. Isaiah and Rick murmured together quietly. That left me to wrestle with my own thoughts. As much as I wished to restore my mark and gain the favor of the goddess, I couldn't wait for her to change her mind.

Rick and Isaiah stood, startling me out of my reverie. Isaiah and I followed Rick out the door, leaving the pack members behind. None of them made as if to follow us. Thankfully, it appeared this ritual was going to be private.

Ophelia had beat us to the waterfall, in spite of us leaving less than 10 minutes after she left the room. She took stood on a flat boulder, drawing a circle with black chalk. We stood quietly and watched her place candles at intervals around the sooty line. She removed some other items from the black velvet backpack she had carried earlier, setting them at specific points around her. Less than two minutes later, she stood and looked towards me. Preparations were complete.

She beckoned to me and I climbed atop the boulder with trembling knees. At her direction, I sat cross-legged in the center of the blackened circle, my eyes focused on the flickering candle flame in front of me. She handed me a smooth black rock and told me to hold it in my left hand. For my right hand she gave me a jagged white crystal.

"I will perform the ritual. You need only to complete a couple of tasks at my instruction. Do not hesitate and do not take long to complete them. If we interrupt the ritual, we will have to start again." She turned to the two men. "Neither of you are to enter the circle for any reason. If you do, the consequences could be disastrous. Not only will it foul the magic, one or more of us could be mortally injured."

My stomach turned to water as she spoke. I hadn't considered the idea that this might be dangerous. Refusing to let fear get the best of me, I swallowed back the bile climbing my throat and gritted my teeth. Nothing was going to get in the way of me being able to defeat the evil spirit.

Ophelia walked the circle, sprinkling dust as she chanted. The wind rose around us, the rushing sound drowning out even the roar of the waterfall. Ophelia continued to walk, her dress remarkably unaffected by the gusts around us. The candles, too, seemed impervious to the wind. She came to a stop in front of me, facing away from me.

"Leah, in your left hand, take the obsidian stone and hold it to your forehead."

Following her instructions, I felt a chill settled over me. Closing my eyes, I focused on the sensations that appeared to be carried to me on the wind. She continued chanting, her words sounding as if they came from inside my head instead of through my ears. I lost track of time as she continued.

Minutes passed as she chanted. I let them flow through me until I heard her call my name. At her instructions I stood, and Ophelia placed both her hands on my shoulders, then pressed her forehead to mine where I had held the rock only moments before. I could feel something sliding along my insides, as if fighting to get out.

"You can open your eyes. I am going to step

outside the circle. When I do, grip the quartz in your right hand until you begin to bleed. Walk the circle counterclockwise, using your blood to extinguish the candles. When you have finished, the ritual will be complete."

Nodding to show her I understood, I waited till she left the circle. My fingers wrapped around the crystal, its jagged edges poking into my skin. Despite the sharp planes, it took considerable force for the blood to begin to flow. Orienting myself in the correct direction, I stopped at the first candle, hovering my bloody hand above the flame. It took three drops before this one went out.

Each subsequent candle took more blood to extinguish. By the sixth and final candle, my death grip on the crystal had my bones aching. Deep red blood ran in a rivulet down my palm and still the candle burned. The storm of sensations inside me buffeted like a ship amongst the waves. Fear that I would not be able to complete my task rose inside me.

I ground my flesh against the points, shifting my hand to make the wounds deeper and wider. I knelt before this final candle, lowering my arm until the flame danced against my skin. Finally, as the well of melted wax filled with my blood, the candle went out.

The wind ceased immediately, and I stood still, clutching the stones in my hands. Unsure of my next step, I looked towards Ophelia. As I did, I caught the look of fear on Isaiah's face. Rick's expression was carefully blank.

"Take the stones to the stream and wash them. Wash your hands as well. Then bring them back to me and collect the candles."

For some reason, I had expected to be weak, but I found the opposite to be true instead. The power surging inside me was both foreign and familiar at the same time. It had the same taste as my mother's magic, but in a subtly different way. Looking down at my hand, I noticed the stone in the garnet ring she gifted me had cracked in half.

Once the cleanup was completed to Ophelia's specifications, we began our trek back down the trail. I showed her my mother's ring.

"Did I ruin her gift of magic by performing the ritual?"

"I cannot say. There is no reason you could not

hold both, being as they are of the same origin. Perhaps there was simply too much for the stone to hold."

"This new magic is strange. It is so similar to my mother's."

"Perhaps in some way you drew on her magic as we completed the ritual, and that is why it seems familiar. Spirit magic is unique to each wielder."

Acknowledging her explanation, I marveled at the new sensations running through my veins. That simple ritual had taken me from feeling inconsequential, incapable, and weak, to confident and powerful. More so than I had felt before, even with the magic gifted to me by the mark. While I knew it would require practice to become proficient, I could feel the success in our future. No longer did I feel my grandmother could squash me like a bug.

CHAPTER EIGHTEEN

My feet practically danced down the trail of their own accord. It took all of my self-control to stay with the group when I felt like I wanted to run through the woods and be free. As we returned to the village, we found the pack waiting in the clearing for us. Most, if not all, knew what we had been doing.

With the knowledge of what happened with the Western pack, we were all in agreement that we should return to aunt Aimee's house and consult my mother. Between her and Ophelia, I would have the best chance of learning to use my newfound magic. Since our family had wielded both types, I believed the books in the attic could be of use as well.

I looked toward Rick. "Do you think we should all go? And by all, I mean the rest of the pack as well? I don't think my mother would mind."

Rick slid a glance toward Ophelia and back to me. "I think it might be safest if we stay together for now."

Ophelia nodded her assent. "Things are moving quickly now, and the evil spirit appears to be getting desperate. We do not want to leave anyone unprotected."

"Aunt Aimee's house has enough protection for us all, at least for now."

Isaiah and I agreed to wait in the clearing while the others grabbed the items they would like to bring with us. As I looked at the cabins surrounding the clearing, I hoped desperately that the evil spirit would not burn their village to the ground while nobody was in it. Her cruelty appeared to know no bounds.

Although it seemed to take forever, in less than

fifteen minutes, the entire group was ready to go. Rick, Isaiah, and I took the lead, with Ophelia right behind us and the rest of the pack falling in line behind her. I studied Rick's back as he moved surefooted along the trail, imagining him finding his way to visit his wife in secrecy.

A sharp stab at her deception brought my excitement down a notch. The weight of knowing just how deeply my childhood had been steeped in secrets hung over me like a cloud. Even if it had been for a good reason, knowing she lied to me hurt worse than most of the other things I had discovered since coming to the sanctuary.

Isaiah reached out and touched my arm. "That's an awfully deep sigh I heard. Are you okay?"

"I'm all right. There's just so much going on in my head at the moment, it's hard to make sense of it all. I barely know whether I'm coming or going."

He pressed his lips together before answering. "I might not be able to say that I know what you're going through, but I'm willing to listen either way. Whenever I can do to help, just ask."

I gave him a half smile. "It's not like you don't

also have a bunch of rocks raining down on your own head right now."

"That's an interesting way of putting it. Sometimes, it feels scarily accurate. Let's just hope that from here on out, the rocks are more the size of pebbles than boulders."

"Or pine cones?" Remembering the day on the bank of the stream, I suddenly wondered how my little chipmunk friends were doing.

Each of us drifted off into our own thoughts. The majority of the pack walked in silence, although I occasionally picked up soft murmurs from behind us. Rick pushed on ahead of us, secure in his assumption that we would all follow. I didn't notice him looking back a single time for the entire hike.

We made quick work of the long hike during the daylight hours, arriving at the clearing surrounding aunt Aimee's house much quicker than I had anticipated. Rick stopped just inside the treeline. Energy prickled along my skin. Something was different.

My eyes scanned the darkened house while I reached out with my senses. Whatever was wrong wasn't obvious, and yet it was clear things weren't as they should be. Worry clenched my stomach. Refusing to wait a moment longer, I strode across the clearing and up the back steps. Rick and Isaiah followed me.

The unlocked back door swung open as I turned the knob. Silence greeted me.

"Mom? Are you here?" My inquiries were met with more silence.

Rick laid his hand on my shoulder. "Let's be cautious as we enter, just in case."

"She's probably napping. Or maybe she went down to the room in the basement. We can check down there if we don't find her on the main floor."

Isaiah motioned to the rest of the pack to cross the clearing and join us. The guys quickly settled them in the living room while I walked down the hall in search of my mother. Each time I called out for her sounded a little louder in my own ears. Where could she be?

The bedrooms and bathrooms were empty. Yanking open the door, I thundered down the stairs to the basement. Flicking the switch at the bottom of the stairs illuminated the basement, showing me she wasn't there either. In my hurry to reach the sacred door, I stumbled, splitting my knee on the rough floor. Despite the blood soaking my pants, I had to look inside. She had to be in there.

The door swung open easily at my touch, revealing that she wasn't in there after all. "Mom! Where are you?"

Pivoting with the intention of running back up the stairs, I ran smack into Rick. He grabbed my arms gently. "Slow down. We'll find her."

"Where could she be? It's not like she had anywhere to go." All of a sudden, I had a thought. The attic!

Pushing around Rick, I ran up the stairs down the hall and into the attic door, Isaiah sharp on my heels. The door itself wasn't latched, and the stairs were dark. Reaching in, I flipped the switch with no response.

Weird. The light bulb must be out. Calling a globe of light, I sent it into the stairwell.

Rick had caught up to us by this point. "Leah, please let me go first." The lines etched in his forehead were deep, raising my suspicion.

"Why?" I attempted to push through the doorway, only to have Isaiah hold me back.

"Just let him, Leah. Please."

"What's going on? Why won't you let me go up there?" My voice became more shrill with every word. I refused to acknowledge the fear sitting like a brick in my stomach.

Isaiah wrapped his arms around me as Rick ascended the staircase. Shrugging him off, I dashed up the stairs, hot on Rick's heels. As I reached the top, he turned back to me, grabbing me in a bear hug. His arms couldn't keep my eyes from the sight.

A low, keening wail escaped my lips. My knees buckled. Rather than try to keep me standing, Rick bent his knees and lowered us both to the floor. I kicked at him, crawling across the rough wooden floor. My mother's body lay in a pool of blood, and everything else in the attic had disappeared.

Rick and Isaiah tried to lift me as I clung to her body, screaming her name. Hot tears poured down my cheeks.

"No no no no no no." I gasped for air, choking on my English. "This can't be happening. This is all my fault. Why did I leave her here alone?"

"Leah, this is not your fault. Please, come downstairs."

All I could do was shake my head. "I can't leave her here. I can't." I turned my head towards the doorway, sensing Ophelia's presence. "Please," I implored her. "Do something. There has to be something you can do."

"I am so sorry, Leah. I can do nothing. Even with my powers, I cannot reverse death."

I screamed at her. "There has to be something!"

At that point, Isaiah lifted me off the floor, cradling me in his arms, and headed for the stairs. My kicking and screaming did not deter him; he handled me as easily as if I were a tiny child. Giving up, I buried my head in his chest and sobbed.

Someone told the other pack members what happened. Each of them stood and began to help. Isaiah sat with me on the couch, ignoring the blood I smeared all over him, and let me cry. My whole body felt as if someone had yanked the bones out. I had no strength, no muscle control, and no desire to ever get up again.

At some point, Ophelia returned to the living room and held a murmured conversation with Isaiah. Before I could ask her any questions, she reached out and brought her finger to my forehead. Her touch brought with it blissful blackness.

Ophelia put me into such a deep sleep that even the evil spirit could not pierce her spell. As I lay unaware, the rest of the pack remained busy. Each of them stepped up to do what needed to be done. Each item they took care of was one that I did not have to cope with.

Darkness came and went before they roused me from my slumber. My eyes opened to find myself in my own room, with Isaiah perched on the end of the bed. Sorrow strained his expression. For a brief moment, I forgot why they had put me to sleep in the first place. Seeing the sympathy with which he looked at me brought it all back.

"It wasn't just a nightmare, was it?"

"I'm so, so sorry." He shook his head. "It wasn't."

"Where is she? We can't just leave her lying on the floor up there, alone."

"Rick and Ophelia have prepared her for the

funeral. The entire Western pack is waiting just outside the clearing."

His words jerked me bolt upright in bed. "They're here? Is there fighting?"

Isaiah shook his head as he rested his hand on my leg. "No fighting. Whenever there is a death in the sanctuary, all grievances are put on hold. There will be an uneasy truce while she is laid to rest."

The very thought of putting my mother and the cold, hard ground so soon after burying aunt Aimee was enough to break me. The dirt over Aimee's grave hadn't even settled yet. My only consolation was that they would be right next to each other for the rest of eternity. Somehow, I knew that wherever they were, their differences would be resolved now.

"I don't know if I can do this." The whisper came out so softly I might not have been able to hear myself had I not already known what I was saying.

Isaiah reached out, and I crawled into his lap, once more shrinking into his arms. How much more could I stand to lose? How much more was the evil spirit, my own grandmother, going to try and take from me?

Anger bubbled up inside of me, pushing some of the sadness away. How dare she? She killed her own two daughters. Her own flesh and blood. Her end goal was to kill me as well. I couldn't let that happen.

Fierce protectiveness for the sanctuary and those who lived there built a wall up around my heart. I needed this anger and this purpose to keep it from shattering. If I let my grief overtake me now, she would win for sure.

With a quivering sigh, I lifted my head. "I need to get up. I need to do something."

After a quick squeeze, he released me. "Let's go down and get you something to eat. We can make a plan and catch up with Rick and Ophelia in the kitchen."

As much as I knew I didn't want to eat, I had to. My logical brain knew that without sustenance, I'd fall apart faster than a piece of bread in the rain. So, despite my own hesitancy, I stood and let him lead me down the hall. The strength of my legs surprised me. I'd been certain they would give out the second I put weight on them.

Two of the members of Rick's pack, whose names

I had forgotten, stood in the kitchen preparing a breakfast spread. Both of them gave me soft smiles before returning to their tasks. Rick and Ophelia sat at the table talking strategy. As I entered the room, Rick stood.

He gave me a warm hug. "Leah, I'm so sorry. While you were resting, we have been cleaning up and preparing for her funeral. I took the liberty of having a couple of the pack members prepare for her burial."

"Thank you. I assume at this point you were able to visit Aimee's grave?"

He stilled briefly before answering. "Yes, I saw it. Thank you for placing her to rest here."

"I wouldn't have dreamed of putting her anywhere else. The sanctuary was her heart and soul, and this was among her final instructions." Tears clogged my throat, making it hard to force the last words out.

Together we stood silently, united in our grief. My mother had never told me how well she knew Rick, but I knew he felt his wife's loss acutely. This had to be devastating for him as well.

"Before I eat, can I see her?"

"Absolutely. Ophelia has cleaned her up and placed her on the bed in her room. Do you want me to come with you?"

"Thank you, but I'd like to be alone with her for a few minutes."

The hall seemed both too long and too short, bringing me to her bedroom door before I was ready. My hand hovered above the knob, not quite willing to turn it and push the door open just yet. Somehow, I knew that once I saw her lying there, it would be real. The previous day seemed like a bad dream, one I could pretend hadn't really happened. Once I stepped over the threshold, there would be no denying it. My mother was gone.

With a deep breath, I shoved the door open, and my eyes landed immediately on her face. No trace of the trauma she had suffered remained. She could have been sleeping. Her face was so peaceful. Stepping inside, I closed the door softly behind me, shutting out the sounds of breakfast back in the kitchen. It took every ounce of determination I had to cross the ten feet to her bedside.

Once there, I dropped to my knees and buried my

face in the coverlet. My grief sucked the strength from my body. Like a small child, I crawled up next to her, stretching out beside her. I hadn't lain next to her in years, and this would be the last time I would ever do so.

There was still so much to say. She should've had years left, just like Aimee. Twice now, the evil spirit had stolen someone important from me. I'd be damned if she was going to get the opportunity to do it again.

Time passed as I lay next to her, holding her cool hand in mine. Sometimes I whispered to her, and sometimes I lay in silence. It devastated me to know there was no way to bring her back. I would, however, get justice for her.

Squeezing her hand one last time, I made her promise. "Mom, I'm so sorry. I'm sorry for everything. This shouldn't have happened to you. I promise you, no matter what it costs me, she will pay."

Climbing out of the bed, I took one last look at her peaceful face, the first face I had seen when coming into this world. Bending down, I kissed her forehead softly. Today, we would escort her to her final resting place. Tomorrow we would prepare for war.

CHAPTER NINETEEN

With a deep breath, I opened the bedroom door, then closed it softly behind me as I strode down the hallway. The faces gathered in the kitchen turned my way as I stood in the door frame. Isaiah got up and came to stand beside me. Rick studied my face closely.

My resolve to be strong from the moment before wavered. The words I wanted to say to them fled my brain and were nowhere to be found. Instead, I opted for a quivering smile.

"I won't let her death be in vain. Aimee's either.

I'm going to protect the sanctuary and defeat the evil spirit with your help."

Smiles and nods came from those in the kitchen. They wanted to return to life as close to normal as possible, just as much as I did. While my life might not ever be the same, I certainly didn't want to spend the rest of it looking over my shoulder to see if my evil grandmother was trying to murder me.

Ophelia stood and offered me her chair at the table. One of the women who had been cooking breakfast earlier brought me a plate. Isaiah made me a cup of coffee, setting the beloved unicorn mug in front of me. The side of it brought fresh tears to my eyes. It sat before me as a symbol of all the love and happiness I had found here. It also gave me hope.

Rick turned my way. "We will have the funeral at sunset, as is our custom, if that's okay with you?"

"Absolutely. I've never been to a funeral, so I don't know how they work."

"Unfortunately, we've had a few. I can say a few words if you'd like, or you can do all the talking. There is no hard and fast rule. We are honoring your mother, so however you'd like to do that is what will do."

"I feel like I should practice what I'm going to say, but I just don't know if I can."

Isaiah rested his hands on my shoulders. "I know that whatever you say will be heartfelt. You cannot do your mother wrong, whether you practice or not."

The remainder of the day passed in a blur. In spite of the activities happening, the house remained shrouded in a respectful quiet. Out the windows, I occasionally caught a glimpse of members from the other pack, but they did not enter into the clearing. At one point, I saw Aaron standing at the trail-head staring into the window. The desire to march outside and kick him in the balls was hard to ignore.

About an hour before sunset, Ophelia approached me and asked me if I would like to help with the preparations to move my mother's body. I hesitated, unsure if I could handle it, but not wanting a stranger to do it either.

"Why don't you come with me? You can participate in whatever you like or just watch."

"Thank you. I feel like I should be involved, but it's suddenly becoming all too real."

As we entered my mother's room, I could see she had already made some changes. My mother lay dressed in a beautiful golden robe on a sheet of black silk. Her hands were crossed and laying on her stomach. Once again, if I had known better, I would've thought she was just sleeping.

"With your permission, I'd like to place some runes on the body. They will be mostly for peace and protection."

"I'd like that. Thank you. Thank you for everything you are doing."

She gave me a somewhat shy smile before beginning. In order to give her space to work, I moved to a corner of the room. Using only for her fingertips, she traced the symbols across my mother's forehead, and the backs of her hands. She then moved to her bare feet and repeated the process. The marks glowed briefly before becoming invisible.

Isaiah knocked on the door before poking his head in. "Everyone is gathered outside if the two of you are ready?"

Was I ready? Of course I wasn't. Did I have a choice? Again, no.

"I guess I'm as ready as I'll ever be."

Ophelia gestured my way. "Would you like to help me fold the sheet?"

Joining her at the bedside, I followed her instructions as the black sheet enveloped my mother's body, tied with satin ribbons in a crimson red. Being unable to look upon her face made the transition somewhat easier. It helped pretend this wasn't really my mother we were about to bury beneath the earth.

Isaiah preceded us to the graveside and every member of the two packs waited respectfully as we transferred my mother's body. With Ophelia's magic in use, there was no weight to carry. We simply guided her to where she needed to go.

The gaping, raw hole in the earth almost undid my vow to be strong. In a beautiful show of respect, the floor of her final resting place had been covered in a layer of rose petals in a pristine white. Rick stood at the far side, and I took a place opposite him as Ophelia floated her body down gently. Isaiah stood silently next to me and took my hand.

A sob escaped, and I pressed my fist against my

mouth to fight it back. Rick addressed the group as I attempted to get myself back in control. His words were beautiful, and he spoke eloquently about someone he didn't know very well. Before I was ready, my turn came.

After sniffle and a hard swallow, I began. "Thank you all for coming here to honor my mother. Many of you did not know her. In fact, there are many of you that barely know me. And yet, here you stand to help me say goodbye to one of the most important people in my life."

Before continuing, I looked around at each of their faces. Most of them were familiar, although there were a few people I didn't recognize standing towards the back.

"As you all know, this is my second loss in a very short period of time." I gestured toward Aimee's grave, which had been included in the circle as people gathered round. "Obviously, losing my aunt Aimee had been unexpected. Never did I imagine that when my mom and I came here to deal with Aimee's death, that I would lose her, too."

"They were the last of my flesh and blood, the

only two people that remained on this earth with whom I share DNA. As most of you can imagine, this loss hits me hard. But it's not going to get in the way of what needs to be done."

My gaze traveled the crowd once more. As it landed on Aaron's face, the flashes of blue in his eyes caught my attention. My focus remained on him as I continue to speak.

"Both my mother's death, and Aimee's, will be avenged. The evil spirit has no place here, and I will not allow her to continue to terrorize the sanctuary. This land and its people will be free of her. Those who have enabled her will be ousted, and the rest of us will be able to live here in peace."

With a deep breath to study my nerves, I looked once more at the sheet that hid my mother's form. The time had come to say a final goodbye. While I knew I would talk to her for the rest of my life, these would be the last words I would say to her while still being able to see her.

"I love you, Mom." My voice broke, and I had to clear my throat in order to continue. "I'm so sorry we're doing this today. I'd have given anything to stop this from happening. But all I can do is move forward from here, and make sure she pays. I know you and aunt Aimee are watching over me together. I love you both, and I'm going to miss you more than you'll ever know."

With my last words, I knelt at the edge of the grave. I scooped up a handful of the earth that had been removed to make way for her. Holding it in my hand, I marveled at its texture and warmth. Despite the hardness of the ground, the soil itself was soft, almost fluffy. My fingers parted and I let it filter through, watching as it dropped onto the rose petals below.

Reaching out, I grabbed Isaiah's hand, and he helped me to stand. Knowing I couldn't watch them throw the dirt on top of her, I turned back towards the house. Aaron came walking up to me.

"What do you want?"

"I came out of respect for your mother, because it is our way." The blue left his eyes and, for a moment, he seemed to return to himself. "Perhaps you should go before something awful happens to you, too."

My fists clenched. Never before had I wanted to

hit something so badly. Isaiah's hands tightened on mine, silently asking me to be calm. "I will not leave."

The blue shot through Aaron's eyes once more. "Then you will be sorry."

Before I could utter another word, a chitter-chattering came from the porch. One of the tiny chipmunks scurried up Aaron's leg and began attacking his face, biting and scratching him. He screamed and attempted to shove it away. His first couple of tries were unsuccessful, and the small rodent drew blood in multiple places.

After a particularly savage bite to the ear, Aaron was able to dislodge it. The poor little animal went tumbling across the clearing. In spite of his injuries, he laughed.

"What have you done to them? Why would it attack you like that? Where is the other one?"

Declining to answer me, Aaron turned on his heel and strode away, wiping the blood from his face.

"I hope those bites get infected!" I shouted at his back.

Isaiah wrapped his arm around my shoulders. "I don't think that there is any doubt he is under the influence of the evil spirit."

Rick joined us, having heard me yell. "I'm not sure what is going on, but I think you're right. This behavior is nothing like him."

Leaving the guys, I strode towards the porch to look for the chipmunk that Aaron had sent flying. I sat on the step as it hobbled towards me. "Poor little thing. What happened to your friend?"

Slowly, as if in pain, the small creature walked over to the spots on the porch that I had identified as blood. It scratched at them and made a low whining sound. My heart broke.

"He or she was injured, wasn't it? I'm so sorry." The chipmunk returned to my side and allowed me to pick it up. Holding it against my chest, I murmured promises to it, too. "I will make her pay, I promise. Are you hungry? Do you want to come inside?"

Standing, I made the assumption that it was, and it did. Busying myself caring for the little creature helped to distract from the fact that at that very moment, earth was being shoveled onto my mother's body. Isaiah and Rick followed me indoors. I made a small nest for the chipmunk with a dishtowel, settling it on the table before going to grab some food.

Rick leaned against the counter as he spoke. "All the members from the other pack have left. There will be no fighting tonight, but I believe they will attack us soon. We do not have much time to prepare."

"I'll work with Ophelia to learn as much as I can. When the evil spirit returns, all I can hope is that I will be ready."

"I hope we're all ready. At this point, we don't have any other choice."

My gaze shifted to the window as I watched the dying light darken in the trees. It felt unsettling to know that the shadows hid members of the other pack. They could be just inside the treeline watching us, and there's no way I would've been able to see them. Just like the evil spirit was still out there somewhere, out of sight, but definitely not out of mind.

Ophelia entered the kitchen through the back door. "The burial is completed. I took the liberty of creating a headstone for both your mother and your aunt. Please feel free to request changes once you've had a chance to look at them."

"Thank you so much. I haven't even thought of those details yet."

She took the chair next to me. "Tonight, I suggest you eat and rest. Tomorrow, we will begin teaching you to master the spirit magic. I will tutor you as best I can. While there is no shortcut to replace time and practice, we will advance you as far as possible with the limited resources we have."

"Can we start tonight? I don't see myself being able to sleep at all."

"Rest is important. What we are about to ask of your body and spirit will require it to be operating at optimum levels. If you do not think you can fall asleep, I will be happy to help you."

A sigh escaped. Knowing she was correct and being accepting of it were two very different things. "I would appreciate your help, if only to be sure that the evil spirit cannot contact me through my dreams. I don't know whether she can see any of my thoughts, but I want to be sure she doesn't get any more information than she already has about our plans."

Isaiah put his hand on my shoulder. "I will stay with you all night. If you become restless, I will know and I will wake you."

"You need to get some sleep, too."

"Don't worry, I'll be able to grab some sleep. What's most important is that you are ready for tomorrow. No pressure, but we're all kind of relying on you."

"Fantastic. Nothing says let's get a good night's sleep more than knowing everybody you know is relying on you to save their life!"

CHAPTER TWENTY

Thanks to Ophelia's magical touch, I slept without interruption. The next morning, I wandered into the kitchen to not only find breakfast on the table, but a stack of books beside it. They were similar to the ones I found in the attic, but had different covers.

Ophelia laid her hand on top of the stack and explained. "While they are not yours, these have been passed down in my family for generations. They cover spirit magic in-depth, which is the magic you are now working with. I think it will help you to read them. So, for now, I'm lending them to you."

I ran my hands along the leather spines. "Thank you so much. I can't tell you how much I appreciate how much you have already done for me."

"Do not thank me until we are successful."

"Whether we are successful has no bearing on my appreciation for what you've done for me so far."

My gratitude made her visually uncomfortable, and she slipped away down the hall. With my left hand, I sipped my cup of coffee while opening the top book with my right. For a brief moment, I stared at the unfamiliar handwriting. My lips turned downward as I thought of the stacks and stacks of grimoires stolen from my own attic. Those books contained my heritage, and I didn't know if I would ever get them back.

Glancing between the book open in front of me and the four other in the stack, I decided to skim them all to begin with, marking the passages I believed warranted a more vigorous study. The first volume held stories and spells, excerpts and explanations. There were lists of ingredients and pictures of crystals with their uses scribbled next to them. Each individual page contained more information than I could ever hope to memorize.

My coffee had long gone cold in the cup when Ophelia returned and asked me if I'd like to go up to the attic and practice. "We will start small and work our way up to more complex things."

"We have to start now. I don't think I have much time to get up to speed." I grimaced as I swallowed the last of the cold brew and followed her down the hall.

We settled on the attic floor after she taught me the basics of creating a circle to contain my lessons. Many of the underlying tenets of handling magic seemed to be the same as that which had been bestowed with my mark. Others, however, required a great deal of concentration. Using the spirit magic sapped my energy much more quickly than my previous form, and I told her so.

"Spirit magic has many forms. Some are lighter, and some darker. The magic gifted to you from the goddess when she gave you your mark was just that, a gift. This magic is being lent to you, and it requires something in return for its use. You will find that over time, you do become stronger, but heed my warning. There is such a thing as too much. Should you cross that line, it will be very hard to get you back."

While I filed that information away in the back of my head, I knew I would step over that line without hesitation if that's what it took. I'd be damned if the evil spirit would win just so I could save a little piece of myself. If the spirits required it, they could have it.

"I understand. At this point, though, we need to do whatever it takes to contain her once more. And that's at the very least."

Ophelia searched my eyes for a moment before continuing on. Two hours into the lesson, my nose began to bleed. She insisted we stop, even though I wanted to keep going.

"Let's go back downstairs, fuel your body again, and perhaps get you more rest."

"I don't have time for those things!"

"And if you push so hard your body gives out, you will be down for hours. Those hours will be lost hours. In this way, you can replenish that which you have taken from yourself, and still continue to practice."

Grumbling, I got to my feet, swaying with the

dizziness. She rose to help me just as I bent over to brace myself with my hands on my knees. Our heads crashed together. She yelped, and I toppled sideways.

"I'm so sorry. I forgot to warn you how clumsy I am." Checking for blood, I rubbed the knot on my forehead, finding none.

She rubbed an identical offending spot on her own forehead, also bloodless. "I am okay. It will heal shortly. That shows exactly why we need to go downstairs and refuel you."

That morning session set the cycle we would follow for the next few days. We alternated between practicing magic until my body was nearly depleted, and then filling it up again. Days bled into the nights. At times, we didn't leave the attic with someone bringing us up a tray of food. Each time I needed to sleep, she used her magic to ensure it would be uninterrupted.

We continued on in this way until she finally looked up at me from the attic floor and said, "I believe you're as ready as we are going to get. What we need now is for you to rest enough to be in tiptop shape. I do believe we will be victorious, but it will cost us."

Her words sent a feeling of foreboding through me. "I'm willing to pay the cost, whatever it is. She cannot win."

"I agree. I would give my life to see her banished from this plane."

"Let's hope that's not necessary." I followed her down the stairs, ramming my elbow into the doorjamb as I shut it behind me. "Ouch! Dammit."

Ophelia giggled. The sound was foreign coming from her, and she pressed her lips together when she saw me staring. "I am sorry. I should not laugh at you when you hurt yourself. It just seems that it happens so often."

Waving away her apology, I sighed. "No hurt feelings on my part. I'm used to it. I've been an absolute klutz for my entire life. I can trip over my own feet and fall up the stairs. My mama used to tease me she should've named me Grace."

The first mention of my mother since her funeral caught me off guard. My chest grew tight and the pain almost drove me to my knees. My hand against the wall was the only thing keeping me upright.

Ophelia pretended not to notice my distress, giving me privacy to get a hold of myself. "I suppose it is a good thing that she did not."

We joined Rick and Isaiah in the kitchen, along with most of the other pack members. Rick motioned for us to take a seat. "I believe the Western pack will attack us soon, if not tonight. Our spies believe they are ready."

Fear turned my insides to icy water. Believing I was ready to use this borrowed magic, and actually feeling confident, were two different things. Looking around the room, I addressed the others present.

"How many other magic wielders do we have besides Ophelia and myself?"

Most of them shook their heads. A young woman spoke. "Most of the pack has only the abilities that come with being able to shift forms. My brother Kenneth and I are the only two with more. Our mother was a sorceress, and she trained us in magic right up until the day she died."

"I'm so sorry you lost your mother." Our eyes met in mutual understanding of that special kind of pain. "And for a second apology, I'm sorry, but I can't remember your name."

"My name is Elizabeth, but you can call me Beth."

"It's nice to formally meet you, Beth. Perhaps you and your brother could join Ophelia and I to come up with some sort of plan?"

"I'm sure he'd be happy to. Let me just go get him."

The others filtered out of the room until just Rick, Isaiah, Ophelia, and I were left. The three of them sitting around that table were the only important people left in my world at the moment. Knowing one of them could be lost in the coming battle almost broke my heart before it happened. I shoved those types of thoughts into the very back of my brain, locking them up in a tiny box to worry about later.

Before any of us could say a word, Beth came tearing back into the kitchen screaming. "They're attacking right now! We have no more time. We need your help!"

Everybody within earshot darted for the back door in a mad dash. Some of the group had shifted already, and others did so immediately upon exiting.

With the door open, I could hear the signs of the fighting from outside. As I rushed to join them, I sent up a quick prayer to the goddess and whoever else was listening.

"Please, please, please. Please let us be successful. Give me the strength to do whatever it takes to come out on top. I will sacrifice anything of myself that you ask of me. I just want to protect this land and these people."

In true Leah fashion, I missed the second step as I rushed to join the fray, tumbling ass over teakettle into the dirt. In an instant, an unfamiliar wolf was on top of me. Ophelia had pushed hard to teach me defensive use of the magic, and I blasted it off me into a tree. A quick glance around told me I wouldn't always be able to differentiate between those that were on our side and those of the other pack. This meant I could not use my magic indiscriminately.

The sounds and smells of the fighting swamped my senses. Snarls of aggression reached my ears on the heels of yelps of pain. The coppery tang of spilled blood was thick on the air. My eyes scanned the area, looking for Isaiah and Rick, wanting to be sure they were safe. My inattention to my immediate surroundings earned me a nasty bite on the arm.

Damien, a bear shifter from the Eastern pack, ripped the offending canine from my arm and eviscerated him with his claws. The urge to lose my last meal at the sight stopped me from thanking him before he was gone again into the fray. Apparently, my tender sensibilities weren't cut out for hand-to-hand combat. Nevertheless, I needed to press on.

After what seemed like forever, I finally caught sight of Aaron about to round the side of the house. Not wanting to let him out of my sight, I sent a blast of energy his way, knocking him off his feet. As he stood, he turned to face me and broke out in an evil grin.

"Well, well, well." The voice that came out of Aaron's mouth definitely did not belong to his body. Just the sound of it caused my heart to stutter.

"Stop right there!"

"Or what, darling granddaughter? Haven't you learned by now that you're no match for me?"

Not wanting to waste my breath on words, I launched into the spells Ophelia had taught me. We'd spent most of our time preparing for just this moment. The evil spirit needed to be removed from Aaron's body and captured.

My first attempt fell flat, eliciting nothing more than maniacal laughter. Focusing my efforts, I blocked out everything going on around me. I couldn't worry about what was happening to anyone else in that moment. If I didn't beat her now, who knew if I get another chance.

Not–Aaron screeched as my magic swelled. The words fell out of my mouth of their own volition. I'd practiced them so many times. Her magic wrapped around me, constricting me so that it was hard to breathe or speak. Still, I chanted. Even as warm blood poured from my nose and stars began to dance before my eyes, I continued.

From my pocket I pulled the small glass bottle Ophelia and I had enchanted to hold her spirit. Falling to my knees, I removed the top. For a moment Aaron's body towered over me, before it too came to the ground with a thud. Opening myself up, I strove to absorb the magic she shoved at me.

Again she screeched. "No! That's impossible!"

Aaron's body lay motionless on the dirt in front of me and the blue wisps of the evil spirit rose from it. She hovered over me, a face eerily forming from nothing. Momentarily shocked by seeing her resemblance to my mom and aunt, I faltered, losing concentration.

Her sorcery bound me with ropes as she laughed. "Do I look familiar, my dear?" The sneering tone of her voice snapped me out of my surprise. "You shall come with me to the temple. There I will sacrifice your body so that your blood will consecrate the sanctuary ground, putting all the power under my control."

"You... can't..." I struggled to answer her with such little air wheezing in and out of my lungs. "Mom banished you."

Laughter floated on the air. "And that's why I killed her. Upon her death the banishment is no longer. She can't control me from beyond the grave."

Anger rushed through me. Asking the goddess for strength, I did precisely what Ophelia warned me against trying. I grabbed all the spirit magic I could hold, then I shoved the last of it all at her. It felt as if my body had shredded itself from the inside. The burning pain ripped through me as blackness momentarily stole my vision.

The moment I could feel her spell being torn from my body as she entered the bottle, I let out a primal scream. The glass vessel in my hand became burning hot as I struggled with the cork. Blisters formed on my skin as her magic continued to try and prevent me from placing the stopper. That act would seal the spell and she would be trapped. For good.

CHAPTER TWENTY-ONE

Fighting against the blackness welling up and attempting to take over, I shoved the cork into the top. With a voice barely above a whisper, I recited the last words that would, hopefully, ensure she stayed in this jar until we found a way to dispel her spirit completely. It took every last ounce of my strength to get those final sentences uttered. Once they were, I lost consciousness.

"Leah! Leah, are you okay?"

The voice sounded as if it was coming from far

away but getting closer. My eyelids felt as if they been sewn shut. My throat was parched, and I felt as if I'd been kissing the sand of the Sahara desert. All I wanted was to sleep for a year. Or six.

Until I remembered where I was and what had just happened. The memory that we'd been in the middle of an all-out war sent me shooting into a sitting position. There was no time for rest; I needed to be helping the others. Hands grasped my shoulders, preventing me from getting up any further.

As my eyes focused, Shelby's face swam into view before me. Blood dripped down her cheek from a gash in her temple. Her left eye was black.

"Thank the goddess you're alive!" She threw her arms around me in a hug.

My ears registered the quiet around me. "Is it over? Where are the others?"

Remembering my last actions before blacking out, I frantically checked the ground around me for the bottle. It lay in the dirt, seemingly harmless, less than two feet from me. Hesitantly, I reached out and touched it with my fingertip, wanting to check its temperature before grasping it fully. At this point, it was cool to the touch.

"It's over, for now. But we need your help. So many were wounded. I know you're tired, but..."

"Of course I can help. Could you help me get up, though?"

Together, we struggled to our feet. As we rounded the corner back into the clearing, I gasped. Bodies littered the ground. Some in wolf form, some human. Isaiah lay sprawled near the back steps. Concerned, I staggered toward him.

As I knelt beside him, his eyes fluttered open. He tried to talk as I pressed my hands against the gaping wound in his abdomen.

"Shh. Let me heal you first."

Gathering more spirit magic was difficult, but I managed. He closed his once more and didn't argue with me, telling me just how badly he'd been hurt. Using enough magic to get the wound closed, and the bleeding stopped, I healed him until he was out of danger, although he wasn't a hundred percent better. Others would need to be healed as well, and I needed to ration the strength I had left.

The next time his eyes opened, the glaze of pain had retreated. "Is she gone? Did we get her?"

Pulling the small bottle from my pocket, I held it up. "We got her all right." In spite of my exhaustion, I managed a tremulous smile.

"You got her. I knew you would."

Rick came stumbling over, with Shelby helping him to stay upright. He faltered as he reached us, dropping to his knees. His eyes rolled back in his head, and I turned to give him my full attention.

"I don't see a wound. What's happened to him?"

Shelby gave him a push so that he rolled over to lay on his stomach. She lifted his bloody shirt to reveal a stab wound. "It's not deep, but it was from a poisoned blade. I don't think he has much time left."

Fear gripped me. Despite my exhaustion, I had to heal him. Frustration gripped me as the spirit magic seem to hover just out of my grasp. With a shriek, I demanded it do my bidding and come to me. To my surprise, it did.

The poison had already spread throughout his body. His systems were shutting down, his heartbeat faltering. In a race against time, I focused on drawing the poison out of him. His shifter magic could heal him if I could get the rapidly spreading poison removed.

When he at last drew a deep, shuddering breath, I knew that I'd been successful. With Isaiah already strong enough to stand, we left Shelby to sit with Rick as I continued on healing those who needed it. Many of the shifters just needed time to heal their wounds, and I focused first on those who had mortal injuries.

As we rounded the far corner of the house, near my mother and Aimee's graves, I let out a strangled cry. Ophelia lay sprawled in the dirt, her dark skirts in disarray. Blood pooled in the dirt around her. Rushing to her side, I shook urgently and called her name.

Deep bite wounds covered her body. So many that even her magic hadn't been able to control the loss of blood. It had taken many wolves to bring her down.

"Open your eyes, Ophelia. Please be okay." I reached for even more spirit magic, attempting to bring her back.

Isaiah wrapped his arms around me and pulled

me close. "I'm sorry Leah, it's just too late. She's gone."

"No. I can bring her back. I know I can. She can't be gone. Not her too."

Tears streaked down my cheeks. I knew he was right. I also knew that I wasn't giving up on her just yet. Reaching out, I smoothed the dark hair from her face. This time, instead of demanding more magic, I asked the spirit gods for a favor. With their blessing, I spoke the words they showed me over her body.

While she did not wake, her wounds closed and her physical body healed. The spell I was granted placed her in stasis. At the moment, I might not be strong enough to bring her back, but I would be soon. With the spirit God's help, I would return her spirit to her body. We weren't going to lose her completely if I had anything to say about it.

"What are you doing?"

I didn't want to admit my plan to him. Not yet.

"Just help me. We need to move her into the attic."

His hesitation showed on his face, but he didn't argue with me. He did as I asked, gathering her into his arms and trekking through the house. While still empty, the attic had been cleaned since we found my mother's body up there, and we lay Ophelia on top of a pallet of blankets in the middle of the floor. Covering her gently, I spoke one last spell over her still form. Here she would wait until I managed to get ready.

Isaiah and I returned to the site of the battle together. Many of the Western pack remained. Together, they pledged their allegiance to Isaiah once more, welcoming him back as their alpha. These were the wolves still loyal to him, and by extension to me.

Along with some help from the pack members, Rick had carried Aaron's form to the back porch and bound him to a chair. "She didn't kill him," he informed me. "However, I think he's going to be out for a while."

"For now, perhaps we should move him into the house. We can take turns keeping watch, just to be safe. Until we talk to him more, we cannot be sure if his behavior was entirely due to the evil spirit influence, or if he chose to be on her side."

He was shifted to a couch in the living room

where everyone could help keep an eye on him. He'd be less likely to get away with something when he awoke with so many sets of eyes nearby.

The remainder of the night passed under a somber cloud. The bottle containing my grandmother's spirit never left my pocket, for fear that in spite of the spells, she could make an escape.

Members of both packs milled throughout the house and clearing, removing all evidence of the battle. All the bodies were taken for proper burial, no matter whose side they had been on. My eyes skimmed their stoic faces, my heart breaking for each of them. Today everybody had lost somebody.

While we were ultimately successful, winning hadn't come without a cost. It seemed anti-climactic in a way. For so long, I'd been struggling with beating the evil spirit, and now it was just over.

The following morning, Isaiah and Rick sat at the kitchen table discussing the merging of the packs. They agreed that the removal of the rogues left within the sanctuary needed to happen immediately. The threats coming from outside the reserve still needed to be dealt with. We couldn't afford to have anyone else helping them from the inside.

Before we could solidify a plan, we were informed that Aaron was stirring. The three of us pulled up chairs and gathered round the couch. When Aaron's eyelids fluttered open, not a trace of blue remained. I studied him intently.

"I'm so sorry." The apology was the first thing out of his mouth.

The three of us observed him silently for a moment, not responding. Rick's face was neutral while Isaiah scowled at him. He looked very much like a little boy at that moment, making it difficult for me to see him as the evil he had so recently been. Still, I wasn't letting my guard down.

"What happened?"

A tear slipped down Aaron's cheek. "I'm not sure exactly how it started," he began. "At first I just sort of realized I wasn't feeling like myself sometimes. I'd feel like I was being watched, even when I was alone. And I started to have periods of time where I couldn't remember what I had been doing. The next thing I knew, you guys were finding me outside the temple. At that point, she wasn't in total control, but she would take over."

He took a deep breath, as if trying to steady his nerves. Both Isaiah and Rick leaned back in their chairs, watching but not joining the conversation. They left me to ask the questions.

"Did you destroy the altar?"

He nodded. "I think that was when she finally took over completely. I could feel she was afraid you would get your mark back. It was like she shoved me into a little box. I was still in there, but I had no control over my own body. It was really strange, watching myself do things even if I didn't want to. When I tried to fight her, it hurt."

Part of me felt bad for him. Another part of me was irrationally angry that he didn't do more to stop her. Isaiah had explained to me that young shifters had even less control than their adult counterparts, so I don't know what I expected from him.

He struggled to sit up, prompting Rick and Isaiah to lean forward, ready to intervene if necessary. He lifted both hands in a show of surrender.

"I'm just sitting up. She's gone now, and I'm not going to do anything."

Rick relaxed and leaned back a little. Isaiah maintained his stance in the chair. Aaron eyed him warily, and then returned his focus to me.

"What happened to the chipmunk?" Rodents don't attack for no reason, and I couldn't bring myself to ask about my mother just yet.

He reached up and rubbed the ear that had received a particularly savage bite. The wounds had healed, but it was obvious the memory was fresh. He shook his head sadly.

"She killed it. I don't know why. I think just to hurt your feelings."

I studied him quietly for a moment. "And my mother?" I bit my cheek while I waited for his answer.

Tears rolled down his face. "I'm so sorry. I tried to stop her." He covered his face with his hands.

Anger surged while I struggled to bring it under control. I wasn't angry at Aaron, not really. I truly believed he would not have harmed my mother as himself.

Gently, I reached out and touched his knee. "Aaron, I know that it was not you." Tears choked me. "No one is to blame for her evil decisions except her."

"But she made me do it. She used my body and my hands. If I hadn't let her take over, your mom might still be alive today."

"Please don't blame yourself. She killed Aimee without any help at all. She is wholly evil, and none of us are to blame for that."

"I hope you can forgive me. I've done a lot of damage in a short amount of time."

Isaiah snorted. I reached over and slapped his arm. "Knock it off."

As angry as I was at my mother's death and wanted someone to pay, I couldn't bring myself to blame Aaron. My focus had to be on figuring out how to remove my grandmother's spirit from our world completely. Even trapped in a bottle with layers of spells, I feared she would find a way to continue wreaking havoc.

We had won the battle, but I knew the war wasn't over yet. Not until she was gone for good.

CHAPTER TWENTY-TWO

Most of the members of the Western pack had gone out to deal with the remaining rogues, as the members of the Eastern pack worked to move their homes and belongings closer. Rick and I made a trip to the cave that held the altar, protecting it with a layer of spells in the hopes that we would once more be able to restore it. Without Ophelia's help, I didn't have the knowledge of how to go about it, even if I felt as if I had enough magic.

As we walked back, I fidgeted with the bottle in

my pocket that held my grandmother's spirit. Fear of her escaping meant it was never far from me. She seemed a little too quiet within her prison, leaving me suspicious that she was planning something else.

"Do you think we'll be able to find and remove all the outsiders and those helping them without our connection to the sanctuary magic?"

"Eventually, yes. They won't be able to hide from us forever. And once they realize your grandmother's spirit is no more, they will have no reason to stay here."

"It just seems too quiet right now. Like I'm waiting for the other shoe to fall."

"All we can do is handle new problems as they arise, one at a time. Don't borrow trouble from tomorrow."

Rick left me on the back porch of aunt Aimee's house while he headed over to meet with Isaiah. As much as I loved her house, it felt lonely and cold when I was the only one in it. It still held so much of aunt Aimee's life that I needed to go through, but because I planned on doing it with my mother, I kept pushing it aside. I didn't see the need to rush now.

Dark spirit magic stirred inside me as I looked at the pile of grimoires Ophelia had left me. They sat in a stack on the kitchen table as if waiting for me. It felt as if the magic itself wanted to be used. Almost as if it struggled against me, keeping it contained.

So far, I admitted my internal struggle to exactly nobody. My desire to prove that I could handle the dark magic had so far outweighed my fear that it would overtake me. Ophelia's warning played itself over and over in my mind. She'd warned me of taking in too much. When battling my grandmother's spirit, I hadn't exactly had a choice. It was either rely on the dark magic to beat her, or die.

As I stared out the window above the sink, I thought I caught a glimpse of Aaron in the treeline. Deciding to invite him in, I poked my head out the back door, but he had already disappeared.

Finding it strange that he would come so close to the house and not stop by, I stepped out onto the porch. The lonely little chipmunk sat on the table eating the crackers I had put out earlier. It began to chatter at me in earnest.

An eerie feeling crept over me. My eyes shifted

toward the sky, looking for the hints of blue that had always heralded the evil magic. Nothing looked out of the ordinary. Jagged yellow lightning streaked across the sky before the thunderclouds opened up and it began to pour.

Escaping the splatter of the rain, I ducked back into the house. Perhaps Aaron would head this way to dry out. Grabbing a cup of coffee, I settled at the table to read. It seemed safe enough to learn as much as I could without actually using the magic to practice with.

Outside, the clouds parted, and the sun broke through, drying the earth. Closing the book, I stood. With a glance at the bottle on the table, I decided to leave it where it sat to go out and visit my mother's grave. It seemed disrespectful to bring the spirit of the one who had murdered her to her final resting place.

Isaiah had made a comfortable wooden chair for me to sit in when I visited. My fingers lightly ran across her headstone as I sank into the seat. Tears threatened to spill over my cheeks.

"I miss you so much, mom. I still can't believe I'm

sitting here talking to your headstone instead of being able to see your face."

The silence of the forest absorbed my words. Every day I came out to the fresh graves beside the house, and every day it broke my heart a little more to see them there. Rick and Isaiah were busy with the pack, and I felt the loneliness acutely.

My fear that using dark magic had unleashed something inside of me kept me from spending more time with the others, despite my desire to be in their company. Until I was sure I had it under control, I didn't want to endanger them.

"Mom, I'm scared. I did what I had to do, but now I don't know what to do with it. I tried so hard to get my mark back, but I fear I've lost the goddess's favor forever."

As usual, there was no response. My palm began to ache where the mark had once stood out against my skin. I used my opposite thumb to rub the area, as I had done so many hundreds of times before. Only now smooth skin met smooth skin.

A sudden, loud, pop and the sound of shattering glass had me jumping to my feet. Terror gripped my heart as I ran up the back stairs. The latch on the screen door resisted my attempts to open it briefly, then flung wide, slamming into my face as it did. Robbing the sore spot, I darted through the doorway.

My eyes locked with those of the semi-familiar dark-haired stranger on the opposite side of the table. He grinned, blood-red lips showcasing sharp incisors, before darting out the front so quickly that I was too stunned to give chase.

Instead, I gripped the table edges, surveying the scene in front of me. Shards of glass littered the tabletop. The vessel in which I had contained my grandmother's spirit was no more.

Searing pain ran up my arm from my left hand. Instinctively, I suspected I cut myself on a sliver of glass. Upon inspection, however, I drew in a sharp breath. Etched into my flesh, in crimson red this time, was the mark of the crescent moon.

A tingle ran down my spine and through my limbs. Apparently, the goddess knew I could not handle this new development without her help.

Using my connection to Isaiah, I reached out to him. "You and Rick had better get back to the house, fast. We have a problem."

* * *

Thank you for continuing to read the story of StarHaven Sanctuary! I cant tell you all what your support means.

As an indie author reviews are the lifeblood of our author business, as many of you know. If you enjoyed the book and feel so inclined, please leave an honest review. The QR code below will take you right to the review page!

ABOUT THE AUTHOR

Tera Lyn Cortez made the leap from voracious reader to author in 2019. In addition to books of every kind, she is a lover of coffee, the ocean, and all things chocolate.

Her home life consists of being a wife and mother to five in the lovely Pacific Northwest, although she admits to being consumed with Wanderlust. Life as a writer allows her to indulge in traveling both our world and those that live only in our imagination when she can't leave her office.

http://www.teralyncortez.com/

http://www.facebook.com/teralyncortez

ACKNOWLEDGMENTS

So many people go into the making of a book that it can be hard to keep track. In addition to my friends and family who encourage me when I'm feeling overwhelmed, I've got the professionals in my corner helping me make these books the best they can be before I send them out into the world.

For the first time I wrote this series from an outline instead of just figuring things out as I go. Thanks, Varun, for helping me with that!

Thank you to Amanda, my editor at Dark Raven Edits, for helping to whip the story into shape and making sure that we get rid of as many of those pesky typos as we can. (I know I always make plenty!)

Do you love this cover? I certainly do! Thank you to Melony at Paradise Cover Design for creating exactly what I wanted, even though I didn't know what I wanted at the time!

YOU ARE ALL AMAZING!

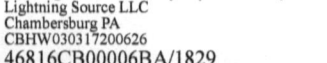